REVENGE

A FABLE

Taslima Nasrin

REVENGE

A FABLE

Translated by Honor Moore, with Taslima Nasrin

THE FEMINIST PRESS
AT THE CITY UNIVERSITY OF NEW YORK
NEW YORK CITY

Published in 2010 by the Feminist Press
at the City University of New York
The Graduate Center
365 Fifth Avenue, Suite 5406
New York, NY 10016

feministpress.org

Originally published as *Shodh* in 1992 by Srishti Publishers in India

Publication of Revenge by Taslima Nasrin is made possible with public funds
from the New York State Council on the Arts, a state agency.

First printing, August, 2010

Cover design by Faith Hutchinson
Text design by Drew Stevens

Library of Congress Cataloging-in-Publication Data
Nasrin, Taslima.
[Shodh. English]
Revenge / by Taslima Nasrin ; translated [from the Bengali] by Honor Moore with
Taslima Nasrin.
p. cm.
ISBN 978-1-55861-659-2
1. Man-woman relationships—Bangladesh—Fiction. 2. Women—Bangladesh—Social
conditions—Fiction. 3. Bangladesh—Fiction. I. Moore, Honor, 1945– II. Title.
PK1730.3.A65S6313 2010
891.4'4371—dc22

2010015312

Translator's Note

The original Bangla title of this book, *Shodh*—an elegant-looking word when transliterated into Roman script—hovers in English meaning, I am told, somewhere between the word "revenge" and the idiom "getting even." I like that balance, and working my way through a basic English translation of Taslima Nasrin's novel, I sought to render an equivalent one between the heroine's suffering and the author's witty feminist commentary on the cruelty of her character's situation. In doing so, I came to understand *Revenge* as a fable—that is, a cautionary tale in which the reader's sense of what is "natural" is challenged.

Take one of the most familiar of Aesop's fables: A tortoise challenges a hare to a race, and the hare accepts, assuming, as we do, that he will beat the tortoise, a creature slow by nature. The impartial fox sets the distance, and the two set off. The tortoise never stops, but the confident hare soon tires and stops by the side of the road to take a nap. He wakes to find that the tortoise has passed the finish line. Slow and steady wins the race, as the saying goes.

Like a fable, the tale you are about to read is a metaphorical narrative, and offers a warning. So as not to give the end away, I won't say what the warning is, but as you enter this story, remember that there are still places in the world where a woman with a physics degree is asked to use it only to boil water, and that even in the West, there are marriages in which a husband's jealousy creates a wife's reality. It is the brilliance of Taslima Nasrin's narrative that the constrictions of sexism she realistically depicts strain credulity as fiercely as the obstacles in any fable. Like Aesop's tortoise, or, if you prefer, like a Jane Austen heroine, Nasrin's Jhumur employs wit and simple logic to get even, and in so doing changes her life and earns a place in the great tradition of clever fictional women.

—Honor Moore
June 2010

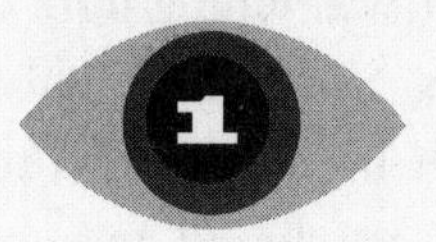

It's dawn and again my stomach is turning, an alien taste spiraling up through me until I feel it on my tongue, a sour dribble flooding my mouth. I make an effort to hold it down, but it keeps rising as if to taunt me. I run to the bathroom, squat at the toilet, and vomit. All day everything sways as I read, cook, or simply stand, hardly able to remember who or where I am. And then I sit or lie down. That's how it's been now, for four days.

Haroon of course hasn't noticed. Even this morning when I approached, a smile curving at the corners of my mouth, and told him I had symptoms of what is surely morning sickness, his eyes remained riveted to the mirror, his fingers busy knotting his tie. I had imagined he would sweep me into his arms and kiss me, or dance me across our bedroom wild with joy, as I had once seen an exultant Dipu whirl Shipra around a dance floor, as if they wished to live a thousand years. When Dipu released her from his arms, Shipra took me aside. She had morning sickness and her beloved husband was in such a state of happiness he'd missed work and they'd spent the whole day alone, celebrating. A husband and wife falling all over each other with happiness! How charming!

But my beloved Haroon kept fussing at his tie. I wondered if he was so inept at achieving a Windsor knot that he couldn't hear what I was telling him, couldn't see my face, my open staring eyes. Nothing I could do broke his concentration. I watched as he inventoried the lunch in his tiffin box for hard-boiled egg, bread and apple, then slid it into his briefcase. And then I watched as he put on his shoes. I'd never seen him so rapt! Not waiting for him to finish, I repeated my happy news, but he neither looked at me nor responded. When he hesitated at the door, I had a flash of hope. Maybe he'll turn and tell me to get dressed for a day on the town, call his office to say he won't be in. "This, my darling, is no ordinary day," I imagined him saying, taking me in his arms. And then we'd broadcast the news to his family and spend the day imagining what to name our first child. Why shouldn't my husband be like Shipra's?

Haroon did none of these things. Once he'd tied his shoes, he picked up his briefcase, and headed to the door. The little smile was gone from the corners of my lips. It wasn't normal for a woman to vomit so early in the morning. I raised my voice so he'd be sure to hear. "Can't you see what's happening to me?" But Haroon kept his eyes on the door, as he answered, "There are some Pepto-Bismol tablets in the cupboard, take them!" I could barely hear him for the image of Dipu and Shipra dancing before my eyes.

"What did you say?" I wanted to be sure Haroon actually understood that I had morning sickness, that he didn't think I was simply down with stomach flu. I wanted to give him a chance to revise his cruel response, to clear his mind, so that he would know what lay in our future, so that he would offer me something other than a pill.

But instead, he slipped through the door, leaving it slightly ajar so I could see him as he walked down the stairs and disappeared. I picked up after him and then set about finishing the kitchen chores just like an ordinary woman. I had been warned never to call after my husband when his back was turned, that doing so was inauspicious, and so I followed tradition, reining in my impulse to shout after him, holding my tongue so as not to bring him harm.

There was, as always, plenty of work: preparing breakfast for everyone, baking the roti that Rosuni, the maid, had rolled out. She was an especially skilled cook, but the family preferred to have me actually produce the meal—another tradition established to prove the worth of a daughter-in-law. And so, even though Rosuni was perfectly capable of it, I chose whether we ate fried eggs or vegetables with our rotis, and thus, everyone was happy, which made Haroon happy. For the six weeks we'd been married, I'd gratified him by preparing meals three times a day, doing all the washing, and taking care of the house, not once allowing the scarf to slip from my head.

But this morning, I fled the kitchen for my bedroom, shutting the door behind me, lay on the bed, arms and legs spread, knowing full well that I ought not to be flouting my duties. But what was I to do? Rosuni was kneading the dough, but I could not stop the churning in my stomach, the rising force in my belly, and the moaning that came whether I wanted it or not.

As I lay there, the beatific expression on Shipra's happy face sailed across my vision, waves of envy breaking on a tiny beach at the back of my consciousness. What was it that had brought Dipu's arms to embrace her, while my news had produced nothing but a pinched look on Haroon's face and the stingy offer of a pill or two? Was my dear Shipra more intelligent than I was, more skillful in the mysteries of love? Even my sworn enemy would agree that I was not one but two notches above my beloved best friend in beauty and talent. Shipra had dropped out of university after a year to marry Dipu. Acquiring pots and pans and every piece of necessary furniture with the perseverance of an ant, she made a home in no time. I too had married for love! And I, too, was living every day and hour in compliance with my husband's wishes, neglecting none of my wifely obligations either in the bed or at the stove! So why, I moaned, why does Shipra get such ebullient love? I couldn't fathom the reason and I couldn't keep myself from weeping.

When Shipra was ready to deliver, Dipu took her to a clinic in Gulshan, despite the fact that his family had wanted him to take her to a government hospital to avoid "unnecessary expenditure." But Dipu was no fool. He knew that proper medical care was not always forthcoming in government hospitals, that one might wait indefinitely for a free bed, that a patient might even find herself giving birth on the floor. Nothing was too good for his Shipra or their child. Dipu did not have the money himself, but he did not hesitate to borrow from his friends.

When I visited Shipra at the clinic before she gave birth, Dipu was always there—fussing over her medication and diet, pouring her fruit juice when she was thirsty. I could barely get close to her! If Dipu wasn't ruffling her hair, he was rubbing his nose against her belly, mumbling endearments: "How is my little one doing in there?" Doctors raised their eyebrows and a nurse, winking, remarked that in her experience fathers were apt to panic rather than purr at the birth of a first child. How I envied my friend, even secretly wishing Shipra and I could change places. If only I were the mother soon to give birth, the woman whose husband was lavishing all this attention!

Again, my stomach churned and again I rushed to the toilet to vomit. No one—not Haroon, nor his Ma, not his brothers or their wives and sisters—no one was willing to acknowledge something was happening to me! That this was the fourth day I'd woken up retching, that my world was lurching, and that, in all likelihood I was pregnant. I pulled myself up from my knees and opened the bathroom door, and there was Rosuni.

I guessed why she was there. It was time for breakfast, and soon the family would want a breakfast cooked by the *bou*, me, the lovely daughter-in-law. But the rotis were not ready, and I was not going to the kitchen that day. Rosuni was the first in the house to notice that something was wrong. She would make the rotis, she said, fry the eggs, and serve everyone exactly as I would. I smiled my thanks and, with relief, threw myself again onto the bed. Soon the sun was blazing through the curtains, scalding my skin, but I didn't care how hot it was, just as long as I could see the sky. So many days, sitting at that window after hours of housework, I'd gazed upward at the azure strip of sky, wishing I were a bird taking flight. If I were robbed of that image of freedom, I thought to myself, I'd be left with nothing.

Some evenings, as a night breeze swept the balcony outside our room, I'd stand longing for a glimpse of the streets crowded with people and moving vehicles, but tall buildings blocked the view, and I could never see beyond the narrow strip of garden. Once in Ranu and Hasan's room, which has a view of the street, I was standing looking out the window when Amma, my mother-in-law walked in, "It doesn't become a housewife to stare at people," she said sternly. "Step back Jhumar, or the neighbors will talk." Of course she reported the incident to Haroon, who quickly sided with her. "You have no sense at all. You forget you are the daughter-in-law, the *bou* of this house."

My dear husband couldn't have been more wrong! I knew I was the *bou* of the house only too well. I didn't dare think otherwise even for a second. I knew that the moment I entered the house I had to reduce my voice to a murmur and keep my eyes lowered, fixed to the ground, so I wouldn't meet the eyes of any other person. How else could I succeed at being Haroon's perfect, self-effacing wife! I'd learned the requirements the day of my marriage when I'd laughed out loud at Haroon's younger brother, Habib, prancing about the house with a cap on his head, and Haroon had come running. "What on earth are you up to? Why are you making such a racket?"

"I was just laughing," I said.

"Don't you know that the people next door can hear you?" What was he thinking? Hadn't I always laughed like that? Hadn't my gaiety prompted him to remark more than once that my sense of humor was what he liked most about me?

"Just laughing?" he said.

"Yes," I said. "Just laughing."

"It's not wrong to laugh," he said, "but you mustn't laugh so loud. You sound like a man!"

Not only did he now disapprove of my laughter, he was at pains to track whatever else I did. Had my head been covered when I stood out on the balcony? He was horrified when I said I couldn't remember. "What will our neighbors think?" he snapped, sounding for all the world like a mother-in-law. "Have you ever seen women staring from those balconies?" he asked, pointing to the apartment building across the courtyard. "A good woman stays indoors," he said. "The more hidden a *bou*, the better her reputation."

So, I would not stand again on the family balcony. Truly, until that moment, I'd had no idea that people in Dhanmundi worried about women on balconies. I'd expected as much in Wari, where my parents lived. In that overcrowded old neighborhood, people poked their noses into the affairs of others twenty-four hours a day. But here, in the heart of the city?

It became a mystery to me what had happened to the man who had courted me. One day, soon after Shipra gave birth, I asked to visit her at the clinic. Haroon raised his eyebrows in surprise. "Why Shipra?"

"Because she is my friend and she's just had a child, and I have given the child her name."

Haroon refused.

"Your life has changed, Jhumar," he said, with a smile on his face I hardly recognized. "Your new life must bear no traces of the old."

"What has happened to you?" I asked him. "I barely recognize you."

"Why can't you figure it out? You are now Mrs. Haroon Ur Rashid, *bhabi* to Hasan, Habib and Dolon. Your address is Dhanmundi not Wari and you no longer carry your old name. It is not proper for my wife to gallivant the entire day! You are the elder *bou* of the house."

Bou indeed, I thought. I remembered the days before we married, the two of us adventuring for days on end and into the night, traveling outside the city. We had walked village pathways and watched the sun drop into the Kansa river, and, sitting on a rocky mount one evening, had watched the stars. I remember Haroon that night. "I want to go through my entire life like this!" he said, his eyes bright, full of love. "I want to talk deeply with you, about the mysteries of existence." I could hardly believe my good fortune. "I hate the struggle of business, the idea of running a household. Oh Jhumar . . . " He seemed never to have his fill. "Why has the day gone so suddenly?" he would exclaim. I too wanted to stretch time. How I looked forward to married life, when the days would extend to weeks in a new life together.

But it was as if the wedding wine had transformed my beloved companion. Dreamy Haroon overnight became someone I did not know. "Work is all there is to life," he would say, standing in front of the mirror, adjusting his jacket. Suddenly he was a cartoon of the working stiff. "One cannot reach the top of the ladder of success unless one works," he'd say, smiling cooly, the door closing behind him, leaving me to hours of loneliness. Gone was my stargazing suitor. Now he was tied to a nine-to-five routine. If I suggested he take a day off, it was as if I'd spoken to him in foreign language. "I cannot afford to lose the money. Those days before the wedding have already cost me."

"Have we no need for each other," I asked him, "just because we are married?"

"My darling, I can have you whenever I want! I know you'll be there when I get home."

Now Rosuni was in my room and, closing the door, she pulled the curtain back. The sun poured down my back. "*Bhabi*, come and have breakfast," she whispered.

"I'm not well, please go away . . ."

She drew close and speaking in a hushed voice asked what was wrong. Her quiet tone reminded me of my precarious position. Even a servant did not want to be caught gossiping with a woman who was failing at her duty. Those with more authority were allowed to be indisposed, but the *bou* had to remain forever healthy. How could she be in a sickbed if someone else got a fever? Rosuni couldn't be seen chitchatting with such a slacker, even if she felt compassion. She had been a *bou* once, constrained to stay in good shape; I could see she understood the drill, her eyes darting toward the door as she made me comfortable, pulling the curtain closed again so I could rest in the shade. I felt a surge of gratitude—in a sense Rosuni and I, maid and *bou*, were in the same boat. Even though a gulf separated us socially, we did the same work—she cooked and so did I, she tidied up, but so did I. As she moved quietly in the half-darkness, I watched her with something approaching envy. She could remove her head scarf whenever she pleased; I had to keep my head covered whether I liked it or not.

I had barely a second for this reverie before Amma burst into the room. Why was Rosuni gossiping with me, shirking her work? "But Madam," Rosuni said quietly, "Hasan is asleep, Habib is out of the house and Ranu is knitting a blanket." She had come to persuade Miss Jhumar to eat. Amma felt my forehead and declared I did not have a fever; Rosuni quickly covered her head and made for the door.

It was past ten o'clock and I was still in bed, but Amma had no sympathy for how I felt. It annoyed her that I wasn't in the kitchen, if not cooking then at least supervising the afternoon meal. Slowly I got up. "I may not have a fever, Amma, but I have a headache and I'm sick to my stomach."

"Headache!" She suffered from it often. "Dousing your head with cold water will banish it soon enough!" she exclaimed. She felt nothing for me I was sure, but I took her advice, making my way to the bathroom to splash some water on my face and neck. I knew she was concerned about Dolon, Haroon's younger sister, whose husband had lost his tobacco company job and was sitting at home. If only Haroon could spare some money and set his brother-in-law up in business, then Dolon could have some peace.

And she was always worried about her other two sons. Hasan, the older one, had dropped out after high school, and Habib had completed his university matriculation only for appearance's sake. Hasan, now living at home, content to eat whatever was set before him, never worried his head over household matters, but a few weeks ago he had appalled us all, producing a thirteen-year-old girl in a red sari whom he proclaimed his wife! The girl, Ranu, was weeping, wiping her tears with a white handkerchief, the red from her lips running down her chin. Who was she? We all wanted to know. And where had Hasan found her? Was she a gentleman's daughter he had kidnapped, or a novice hooker from the red light district?

Haroon and his father attacked Hasan the second he brought the girl into the parlor, setting upon him with their fists, pushing him to the floor. The young girl herself began to howl in fear and horror at the bloody mess her husband had become. What had happened? Words soon tumbled out through a deluge of tears. She had left her military father's house to come away with Hasan, who'd kept her hidden for six months. And then she howled some more. "We are leaving the country," Hasan blubbered, welts and bruises rising on his cheeks, blood dribbling from his nose. "I cannot live here."

Habib was quite the opposite. He had no aspiration to travel. He relished the idea of living in one's own country and carrying on like a lord. Nor did he show any sign of falling in love or preparing to marry. Such traditions, he declared often, were futile in the extreme and bothersome. Strutting through the house, he sang with abandon, strumming the guitar that hung from his neck. He was in love with music, he proclaimed. "Life is short," he'd say in response to any criticism. "One may as well sing or dance!" And sing he did, no matter how his parents worried.

But now Amma seemed more disturbed about the destiny of her only daughter's hapless husband Anis, whose problems she confided in me because she thought I might broach the subject to my husband. But Haroon knew only too well the misfortunes of all his siblings. Night after night, he would sit, lost in thought, smoking one cigarette after another.

"Why do you worry so," I once asked.

"You wouldn't understand."

"Why wouldn't I?"

I had never been successful in convincing Haroon that I was quite capable of coping with the problems that afflicted his family, although I tried reminding him, with added emphasis, that I had been a student of physics. I may cook, but I am better educated than Rosuni, I would say. One night, sensing he would be receptive, I approached Haroon about Anis, and he listened. "Perhaps I could bring him into my firm," he said. "We're collaborating with the Koreans, and I need a new man."

As for Habib and Hasan, I also obediently raised that issue. "It's easy," he said. "I'll send them abroad to earn a living!" But he did not consider me capable of real discussion. There were hours of meetings in the drawing room—he and his parents, brows furrowed, considering the fates of his ne'er-do-well brothers—but I was invited only as the *bou*, gracefully sweeping in and out serving tea and biscuits.

Why, I wondered, had Amma been so eager for my assistance with Dolon's husband? Did she imagine that Haroon, caught up in his marriage, had no time to spare for his family, that her only access to her oldest son was through his new wife? And why was her most passionate concern for me that I cook when I showed all the signs of being pregnant with her grandchild? Yes, there was the custom of the *bou* of the house preparing certain foods, but wasn't it also the custom that the daughter-in-law reproduce?

I pulled myself from bed and entered the kitchen. Garlic, onion, raw fish, and turmeric, smells I'd always loved, suddenly intensifying my nausea. Rosuni had already cut up the fish and onion and measured out the garlic, and Sakhina, the second maid, was grinding the spices into a paste. I steadied myself and set about placing the pan on the fire, throwing in the onions and garlic, turning the chillies and spices. Why, I asked myself, does this family pant for my cooking when in a sane world I could barely qualify as Rosuni's assistant? Was it because my hands were fairer than hers? Because I had gold bracelets while Rosuni wore bangles of glass? Or was it that my knowledge of the great formulas of physics gave me a gift for refining the flavors of Bengali cuisine?

When he got back from work that day, Haroon behaved as if he had no memory of my morning agony. Sitting down for supper, he chattered on about his new Korean colleague, how the gentleman could not speak English, and had conversed with Haroon for an hour in his own language, which Haroon, of course, could not speak and for which he had no respect. He'd arrange for a translator, he said, and then sat down in front of the television to watch Mumazzudin Ahmad, who had cast himself in the role of an absentminded teacher. Haroon laughed and laughed. I would have laughed too, but my head was throbbing.

"I'm sorry," I said. "My stomach again."

"Of course," he said, barely looking up. "You must go and lie down if you feel unsteady."

When he came to bed, I was still awake, and soon he was loosening my sari. I sighed deeply as he began to make love to me. How could a man who was so indifferent to his wife's discomfort be such a sensitive lover? Afterward, Haroon lit a cigarette and blew smoke rings as he always had, as he had in the early days of our marriage when our love was still new. "You see, I'm no longer tired," he said, his entire frame loosened and calm. But I was hardly calm and I'd had no pleasure in spite of the precision of his touch. Haroon had simply used my body to relieve his fatigue.

When I returned from the bathroom, Haroon had stopped smoking. He was lying with his back turned. I lay down beside him. Perhaps now he would listen to me, but when I moved closer to him, the sound of his snoring greeted my ears.

As Haroon brushed his teeth, I vomited. To my surprise he reached for me, and steadying me from behind, gave me some water to drink. Such comfort, I thought, closing my eyes and letting my head rest against his shoulder. Quickly he helped me to our bed, and as soon as I lay down, fetched a couple of Pepto-Bismol tablets. "Here," he said, jabbing them at me. "Swallow them now."

"Will I stop vomiting?"

"Of course." And then he went into the bathroom, only to return minutes later, wrapped in a towel. I watched as he dressed, knotted his tie and touched cologne to his neck.

"I'm not feeling better," I said. "I feel strange."

"How?" Now he was slipping into his shoes.

"I'm pregnant."

At first he didn't answer and then he said, "What rot!" and turned toward the door. In a second he was gone and I was alone with the burning sensation in my stomach, making trips into the bathroom where only moments ago he had showered. How had the charming boy I'd met at the academy musicale become such a cruel insensitive man? How could an accomplished and intelligent man of twenty-two deny that morning nausea was a sign of pregnancy? I remembered our first phone call barely two years before.

"Remember me?" a young man's voice had asked.

"Not really," I replied.

"We talked once in the park . . . "

"Possible, I guess," I answered. "I've talked to so many men, I can't remember them all. What's your name?" I admit I was harsh, but I'd often been harassed by strange phone calls—we all were, my friends and I, in those days.

"What's the point of giving you my name?" he said. "There are scores of Haroons in the world. You must know at least ten!"

I tried to recall him, but I could think of only one Haroon, a distant cousin. This Haroon would not get off the phone, even after I insisted I knew no one by that name.

And then, suddenly, I recalled a man I'd seen, lurking at the periphery of the terrace as my friends and I chatted before a concert. I remembered his wonderfully evocative voice—he'd made an excuse to say hello. With his crisp, starched panjabi and pyjama, he didn't look at all like one of those boys who walked about, rumpled and careless, with the gaze of a poet, a sling bag over his shoulder. Rather, he looked like someone sent from the Ministry of Culture to report back about the quality of the concert. I remembered that Arzu had persuaded me to sing, and when I took up the song, I'd seen the man take note. Soon he barged into our midst and demanded I sing more, encouraging Arzu, Subhash, Chandana, and Nadira to join in.

"Where did you turn up from, sir, that you dare ask me to sing?" I asked. And the boy—perhaps I should say the young man—gave me a beatific smile. He remained by my side even when we went inside for the music. When the soiree ended late in the evening, he was still with me.

"Your singing was a whole lot better than anyone else's," he said, not too quietly. Chandana poked me with her elbow as he disappeared.

"So why's that jerk after you?"

As we walked along the avenue, looking for a tonga, a white Toyota pulled up beside us. "Where are you heading?" It was the young man with the starched clothes and evocative voice. "Let me give you a ride."

"Not necessary," I said. "We'll get a tonga."

"You won't find one. The entire fleet is stationed near the arena waiting for the football match to let out." Still, I tried to get rid of him, insisting we were bound for an old part of town.

"I'm heading there too," he insisted. "I live there too."

And so, in spite of my reluctance, we got into his Toyota. Actually Subhash forced my hand, only too pleased to get a lift. Haroon talked to him most of the way, about the plague of mosquitoes in Dhaka, the impossible traffic in the old city. Then, as we got out, he said, without specifying when, that he'd be honored to hear me sing again.

But I couldn't imagine that anyone would ring me up after such a brief acquaintance. No doubt it was not so easy to locate a phone number, even given the address. But I didn't ask how he'd found me.

I cut the first call short. "I'm busy," I said. But he called the very next day, and the day after that.

"What's up?" I asked.

"Are you annoyed?"

To tell the truth, I wasn't feeling too comfortable about carrying on a conversation with a man I hardly knew, and my experience had always been that I could easily cut off such chatter after an initial exchange of pleasantries. But what was typical didn't seem to work with Haroon. He just kept talking, and about everything under the sun. Anything, it seemed, to keep me on the phone. He was an engineer, he told me, and had started his own business—manufacturing generators—in Savar. He had an office in Motijheel, but he lived in the Dhanmundi section of town with his parents and siblings. He drew a picture of a happy family.

"You owe me a song," he said.

"I beg your pardon!"

"Didn't I see you home the other night?"

"So you're demanding the fare I would otherwise have given the tonga driver?" Haroon's laughter rang loudly in my ears. "It was you who insisted on seeing us home!" I reminded him. "And I told you that I would only accept your offer if you required nothing in return, remember?"

But he would not be deterred. He kept calling, kept asking me to sing for him. He wouldn't accept the notion, for instance, that I sang only for myself, and after a while, exhausted at the intensity of his appeals, I was persuaded first to sing, and then to talk for hours on the telephone. But also, I had become curious.

It wasn't long before he began to ask me to sing this song or that. Tagore's *I lend my ears* or *Far, far away*. And then one day, he begged me to sing, *My heart refuses to calm down* . . . The message was so obvious, I couldn't help teasing him.

"What has affected your heart all of a sudden?" I asked, and Haroon sighed deeply.

"My grief that you are so cruel that you will never understand me." He laughed. "Can't you see that a storm is gathering!" he exclaimed, and asked me to sing, "On such a stormy night, you'll come to me." I stopped after a couple of lines.

"Do you take me for a courtesan? I must sing to please you?"

Now it was Haroon's turn to sing. He wasn't good at it, but he tried, only to get me to sing again, staying on the phone for hours as I sang and sang, then noisily applauding before he exclaimed, sighing, "There's such magic in your voice."

The first three months of our acquaintance took place on the telephone. Our intimacy seemed to soothe both of us. I began to wonder if I was imagining it all, this attraction that seemed so sudden and unexplained. And then one day when we were on the phone, Haroon's tone of voice abruptly changed.

"I don't feel happy going on like this."

"What do you mean?"

"I want to be closer to you . . . "

"Whatever for?"

"For nothing else but to get my heart's fill of you."

"Do you mean you are not happy with only talk and singing?"

"It's not the same as sitting face-to-face."

So we met on the university grounds, and he took me to his office. I was most happy to find a vase of fresh flowers on the table. He spread the flowers on my lap, pinned some in my hair, and cried, "My darling, these roses are meant only for you!" I sat silent, watching Haroon fuss with snacks. "Will you have tea?" "7UP?" "A chicken bun?" I was gazing at his beautiful eyes, at the smile that lit up the corners of his mouth.

Now, of course, we no longer sing, and Haroon looks at me sharply if I begin even to hum a tune, and there is never time for roses. But in those days, he had no compunction about missing work and coming to meet me after my physics class in Curzon Hall. Time and again, I'd come out of class to find a good-looking man with a beautiful smile waiting for me, dark glasses keeping his dancing eyes from my gaze. I wanted everyone to celebrate my good fortune. I was not only a brilliant student and an effective leader in student politics, but I excelled in love as well! And Haroon couldn't have been more solicitous of my achievements and obligations, standing by as I posted slogans and gossiped with friends over tea at the canteen. Afterward, he'd sit me next to him in his car and drive me around the campus, a cigarette dangling elegantly from his lips.

Every so often that spring we drove a great distance, over the bridge of Buriganga, and settled ourselves on the banks of the Dhaleshwari River. Like me, Haroon loved seclusion, and those days alone were our great pleasures—hours of contentment I grew to rely on. One day, as usual, we drove to the river, and after we'd settled at our customary place,

Haroon looked at me with an expression I didn't recognize. I waited as he overcame what seemed like dismay and began to speak. I was not, he told me, the first woman to whom he had given his love. Anguish, like a thin string, tightened around my heart.

And so he'd sat beside the same river in quiet intimacy with another girl, had gazed into the eyes of another and declared his love! Of course I believed I was the first woman who had captured his heart, and, pouting to keep from weeping, I declared, as if it could change what he had just told me, that he was indeed my first and only love.

"Did you come here with her?" My eyes were tearing, but I fixed them on the passing boats to keep my composure.

"Many times."

"Was she beautiful?"

"She was . . . "

I fell silent, and then managed another question. "Did you love her very much?"

"Ah, yes!"

"More than you love me?"

Haroon took my hands and gave them a warm squeeze. "Silly girl, are you angry? I was talking about an old relationship. I loved her once. I don't anymore. I love you now."

What Haroon was saying was not in the least outrageous. I could have fallen in love with someone only to move away from him, and I could then have found another man and come to believe he was the right person for me. Shipra had been in love with someone else before she met Dipu. The relationship had lasted only two years because the boy was an alcoholic. Then she met and fell in love with Dipu and married him. Things can happen that way, I reassured myself.

"Do you think about her?"

"No," Haroon said.

"Do you mean to say that you never think of her? How is that possible? Do you not feel the pain of loss?" Haroon laughed.

"I don't feel anything." Looking straight into his eyes, I tried to determine if he was telling me the truth.

"How can you forget someone you've loved?" I asked impatiently.

"Why not? It's entirely possible."

"Then you will forget me one day?"

"Why are you comparing yourself to her? You're different."

"How? How are we different? She's a woman too. You've loved both of us."

"You don't compare . . . "

"Why not?"

"She wasn't nice . . . "

I can't remember if I felt happy at the knowledge that she wasn't a nice girl and reassured that I certainly was. Now it's clear to me that I shouldn't have felt smug for being praised, but that is exactly how I did feel. Now I've learned that a person who summarily dismisses a former attachment can, given the chance, turn his back on any love. "It was highly improper of you to speak of her that way," I told him much later.

"Judge for yourself," Haroon said. "How could I marry

someone who cares only about cars, money, and jewelry and has no time for music?"

"But people differ in taste and inclination. That doesn't give you the right to defame her. I have no sympathy for your generator business, but I don't criticize you, do I?"

Haroon said nothing, and we never finished the conversation.

But now we are in Haroon's office and I am looking at a bouquet of roses and dusk is descending and we are in love. The place is deserted and everybody is gone and my apprehensions are soon drowned in a rush of love. Haroon kisses me for the first time that day, digging his tongue deep into my mouth, my lips swelling as if stung by a bee. And now he is doubling up with laughter at the sight.

"You look funny, not yourself at all!" he is saying while I try to hide my mouth behind my hand, which he keeps removing to get a glimpse of my swollen lips.

"What are you looking at?"

"Your soft, pure, virgin lips! They are so untouched, they puff up with the first kiss!"

Haroon's eyes were shining with happiness—that I was inexperienced and that he was the first man to touch me thrilled him, but getting home with reddened, swollen lips was unpleasant. I was so nervous I confined myself to the darkness of my bedroom to avoid a barrage of questions. I made all kinds of excuses: I'd eaten already, I had work to do. Sleepless and seized with hunger, I tossed and turned, and the next morning went to Haroon's office as soon as he called. We lunched at Superstar and spent the entire day together. He held me close, as if he were afraid of losing me. And he wanted me, was bent on taking me, an uninitiated girl. It was on that day that part of me first suspected that Haroon couldn't possibly really love me, that I was simply a conquest, that as we sat on the banks of the Dhaleshwari and he proposed marriage, his smile was the smile of a man who had found himself an innocent girl to take as a bride.

But I had no reason to object, I told myself. He came to see me every day, and took me to his friend's house in Gulshan almost every evening. We wanted privacy, which came to us after chatting with Shafik over tea, Haroon stealing a kiss every time his friend's back was turned. We walked meadows and forests, and saw the sights, often in the company of our friends, and whenever we neared Savar, Haroon made a dash to his office.

But he never took me to his family's home. He didn't want them to feel I was someone they already knew, he said. He would surprise them by introducing me as his bride. We couldn't manage for long just visiting friends, so we sought seclusion at my family's house in Wari. But that was no better. My parents were there, my sister burst in whenever she wanted, her little girl climbing onto Haroon's lap. The dog never took to Haroon, howling whenever he appeared, and geese and hens wandered freely through the living room as my beloved sat helpless amid the chaos. He wanted privacy, and clearly, I could not provide it.

"You seem to enjoy being bored to death," he said.

"What do you find exciting?"

"A kiss, a cuddle, the soft feel of your breasts."

My body trembled. I was young and easily excited, ready to fall headlong in love. I liked all of Haroon, my misgivings overcome by the power of new desire. I shivered at the brush of his arms as he drove me around, keeping his right hand on the wheel and not letting go of my hand even once, not even when he shifted gears. How I wished I could prolong the momentary rush of holding hands! I felt so inadequate as Haroon fell over me, hungry as a tiger mauling a doe, delving deep into my body.

We continued in much the same way through the spring, both of us believing ourselves ready for marriage, neither of us with another candidate in mind, but it took a shove from the outside to bring us to the actual ceremony. In the weeks after graduation, I was hardly idle. Though I had graduated I was still active in student politics. "Is there any need for you to be so involved?" Haroon asked one day.

"What do you mean?"

"Your party will never win," he declared, "no matter what your effort."

"I have my ideals," I retorted. "I don't need to abandon them, even though Shibir is bound to win."

"Honestly," he said, "women aren't of much use."

"What do you mean?" I was startled.

"I mean, women are fit for singing but not much else."

"But you yourself are fond of singing!"

Haroon did not elaborate and unfortunately I did not draw him out. Perhaps if I had, his present behavior would not have come as such a surprise. Perhaps I might not have married him. But passion had taken hold.

We had little time to ourselves, and often, to be alone together, we stayed out late at night.

Seeing all this, my father called to me one evening, and, with a brittle sharpness in his voice, declared, "Either marry Haroon or stop seeing him!" I was completely taken by surprise. "I don't want to find that boy hanging about my house and the two of you spending all that time together without a betrothal," he said. "It's not proper."

"I'll marry when I'm ready," I said.

"When will that be?"

"Maybe in six months." Haroon and I had talked about waiting six months, but now my father was shouting. "What difference will another six months make?"

I didn't want to argue. Mama had warned me not to aggravate Baba's poor health. "Heaven knows what will happen if he gets too worked up," she muttered. "The poor man almost had a stroke waiting for Nupur to marry."

And so, a few days later, I announced to Haroon that I was ready to get married. He was totally unprepared. Some weeks before he had scolded me for putting off our engagement. "Time and time again, you give one excuse or another," he'd said. That was when we'd decided on the six-month wait. That day he had wanted to take me straight to his house in Dhanmundi whether I was ready or not. Now he wanted to know what my hurry was.

"It's Baba," I said. "He doesn't want us so close without marriage."

I understood what really lay behind Baba's concern,

but I couldn't tell Haroon. My only sister Nupur had had a love affair with a well-to-do young man named Akram, who came and went whenever he chose. He'd endeared himself to us all, becoming one of the family. We waited and waited for him to propose to Nupur, even planned the menu for the wedding, Akram butting in, "Just meat won't do, we must have fish and fried brinjals as well." He'd enjoyed those dishes at his friend Sanjib's wedding.

"Why not have stuffed taki fish, crushed dry fish, prawn malai curry, hilsa with mustard and fish fry. Why not have all of that to go with the rice?" he asked.

But Akram never married Nupur. He left her after five years of courtship, and Baba was so hurt he regarded any suitor with suspicion. One day, he was certain, Haroon too would disappear, and again he'd be left with a daughter out in the cold.

My family was not rich, but we were by no means poor. Baba had sent both his daughters to university and taken care of our desires. At first Nupur decided to remain a spinster, but when she changed her mind, Baba found Dulal, a fine man with a fine job, and they married. Nupur had excelled as a student of Bengali literature, but now she was an accountant—the irony of it all! Within a year, they produced a daughter who drove everyone mad, but they were happy.

I wondered what made Baba insist I marry Haroon right away. I'd received several marriage proposals he had turned aside, but now he was in a hurry. Had he lost faith in my ability to attract a proper husband? What if I didn't want to marry Haroon? Baba's sudden declaration hurt my feelings.

Why didn't he see me as an attractive and intelligent woman any man would desire?

In any case, within two weeks, Haroon and I married with little ado. There were no arguments over fried brinjals, we just gathered a few friends and that was that. I showed Baba that I was a proper woman, and that Haroon was no mere fling, which brought me some satisfaction.

Life changed abruptly when I entered Haroon's house. His parents objected immediately to my calling him by name, insisting that I call him by the old-fashioned honorific. I had a hard time switching, but Haroon was on their side. "Just don't address me by name when they're around." So I stopped calling him Haroon in front of the family. After that first surrender, I noticed quickly that even when we were alone, I was unsure of his attention. 'Are you listening?" I'd say.

No longer did he take me out to visit his friends or roam the city. We came together only with his family. With my head covered, I followed my husband into the houses of his relatives, showing due respect to elders. At my parents' house, I had rarely been required to touch anyone's feet in reverence, but Haroon insisted I change my ways, and solemnly, I did exactly that.

Now he slammed into the room, breaking my reverie. I told him the pills had not worked and that I was still sick to my stomach.

"How can that be?" he said.

"I have told you what I think," I said.

"And what is that?"

"I'm pregnant."

"Impossible," he said, "and just because you think you are—"

"Why do you say it's impossible? Take me to the doctor. Let him decide!"

"You make a fuss over nothing," he said, "running to the doctor at the slightest excuse!" And then he marched into the dining room and ate in silence, watching television.

Alone in the dark, I stood at the open window, the dingy night sky throwing murky shadows into the room as I listened to my breathing, keeping my eyes wide open.

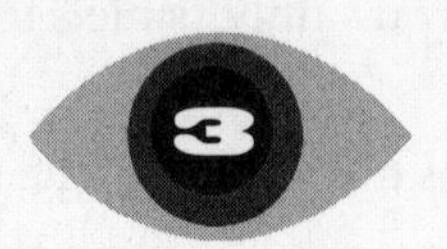

It was becoming Haroon's habit to depart for work without breakfast, leaving his tiffin box lying on the counter, and so I wasn't surprised the next morning when he rushed out the door, hardly pausing to respond when I asked if he planned, again, to lunch with a colleague. I was becoming adept at preparing breakfast for the family and gathering the washing for Rosuni. This particular morning I also dusted the living room furniture and, when I finished, found myself again looking out the window and up at the blue sky. There was no end to the free time I had in this house, even with all the cooking and arranging that was my duty as the oldest daughter-in-law. But none of what I did added up to work—Rosuni took care of the heavy cleaning and once in a while Amma would even pitch in. I was superfluous, it seemed.

Standing there at the window, I wondered what on earth I was going to do with myself. I had never been the kind of girl to sit at home, and my inactivity burned like the sting of a poisonous ant. As a child I had the run of our house. My sister Nupur was a docile daughter, but I was a tomboy with no patience. When I was little, Ma once took us to see a fortune-teller. Nupur sat there calmly and listened to the woman's utterances, but I fled to the courtyard, climbed a mango tree and loaded the end of my sari with fruit. This hardly surprised my mother as at home I was apt to play with the boys in the neighborhood, slipping and falling, tearing my clothes on a thorn. I had remained contrary and impulsive and any challenging tree still invited me to climb.

Nupur had visited me a few days earlier. It was easy for her to stop by since she worked in the Dhanmundi branch of the Sonali Bank, just a stone's throw from her house on Green Road and a few blocks from mine. "Why don't you come and see me?" she said as our visit came to an end. I explained that such a visit was not possible, that I was not permitted to go out alone, that I would have to wait until Haroon was free and willing to drive me. Nupur was stunned. How was it that her wild sister had become a cowering wife, a docile woman who would never disobey her husband. "Not only that," I told her, "my husband, my lord and master, is seldom home before nightfall."

"So how do you pass your days?" Nupur blurted, her eyes wide with disbelief.

"Time goes by," I said, purposely avoiding the truth, which was that my hours were as stagnant as the pools left after a monsoon.

Nupur was a couple of years older than me, all the more precious a friend because she'd almost died of typhoid when she was ten. My parents had been sick with worry. "You'd worry even more if your sick child were a son," our family doctor had said one day in my presence. Young as

I was, his remark startled me. It had never occurred to me that a mother and father might love a son more than a daughter.

To be fair, Baba never complained about having only girls. If people expressed pity, he proudly pointed to me and said, "This one is my son . . . she'll do everything a boy would." I took my father's pride in me as permission to do what a son might—run to the pharmacy to pick up medicine or to the market for fruit, run faster than the boys, run interference for my beautiful older sister. Once a boy named Basu wouldn't stop whistling at Nupur, and so I went to his house in the company of my gang of boys, collared him, scattered his books and papers, gave him a few hard blows, and disappeared from the streets for a few days. After that Basu didn't bother Nupur again.

For a few years we were a team, seven boys and two girls. We played marbles, spun tops, flew kites, and played cricket, football, and badminton on the grounds of the house at Wari. Because I ran the fastest, I was the leader of the pack; no one could catch up with me, not even the boys who were a couple of years older. In school, I was always in the first five in my class, something that thrilled Baba who'd come home with a packet of *sandesh*, my favorite pastry, whenever I did well on an exam. "I don't need a son," he'd exclaim, "this girl will become a judge or barrister one day and protect the family honor." Even though I had chosen physics, hardly preparation for a legal career, Baba did not object. "It's an excellent subject," he remarked. I had two opinions about that. I had learned how to place a skillet on the fire so it remained steady and how to adjust the heat so rice would cook, but I had also learned why it cooked! How could anyone say physics was useless!

Baba, naturally, had a university degree, but Ma had been married off at fifteen without even finishing school. And though neighbors expressed their sympathy to her as well, she, like Baba, had no regrets at having two daughters. Even when friends took her aside and urged her to try for a boy, Ma bristled. "Will a boy solve all our problems? He'll take to smoking at thirteen, at fourteen ogle girls outside the school, and at sixteen carry a knife! Girls are much less trouble."

My mother's rejoinder cowed her arrogant advisors, and she was just as bold with us. She always told us to stand tall and even though she'd never gone to school, she encouraged our studies. "I have turned my mind to spiritual matters, my dears," she would proclaim, "because I have nothing else to do. Religion is the preoccupation of those who have no work at hand." And then she'd go on. "I have always lived a life of leisure—almost from the moment I was born. Your lives will be different. Of that I am sure."

Perhaps.

Yet now that Nupur and I were married and now that I was learning what married life was, I wondered how much difference there was between us degree holders and our thwarted mother. Weren't all three of us yoked to the drudgery of running a home? Hadn't my mother once been the *bou* of the house, just like me? In Haroon's home, all my degree gave me was a rather irrelevant superiority to Ranu, the younger *bou*, who had barely finished secondary school, let alone gone to college.

Tears were running down my cheeks. I wiped my eyes, walked to the telephone and dialed Haroon at work.

"What's up," he said brusquely.

I wanted to share my new perception, to declare myself in some way, but all I could manage was, "Nothing really."

"Why on earth are you calling me then?" Haroon was astounded I would ring him up on a whim, and I was astounded that he could forget all the carefree hours we'd spent on the phone before we married. "Don't call me unnecessarily," he barked. "You know how busy I am." Of course I knew—it seemed these days that he had not a second to waste. How could he have changed so drastically? Just as I put the phone back in the cradle, Amma swept into the room and, seeing me doing nothing, began to complain about Abba's arthritis. He wasn't feeling better, she said; in fact he was getting worse. What did she expect me to do about it? Haroon was the person who attended to his father's aches and pains. Haroon would take Abba to the doctor, I suggested. I stood there, my face veiled, sighing deeply in order to show my concern about my dear father-in-law.

"It's not enough just to be a *bou,*" Amma had once announced. "You have to deserve the title." She herself had been her mother-in-law's pet, had singlehandedly run her in-laws' house without any hired help. I could hardly imagine it, looking at her now—she was such a ball of fat, sitting idle most of the day, walking with such heavy steps. Now she was rubbing her back. "I have such aches and pains," she moaned. "I want Rosuni to give me a massage, but then who'll cook our supper?" I knew what she wanted and I went to the kitchen, sent Rosuni right to her, and began the cooking on my own. It was not that I begrudged Amma a massage—I'd done it once. Such a mountain of flesh! That night we sat down to leftovers.

"Why haven't you cooked?" Haroon demanded, making a face.

"I couldn't find the time," I said. "I've spent the entire day pressing the pain from your mother's legs."

"There's a saying in Bangla," Haroon said, irritably. "'A woman who cooks always finds time to put up her hair.'"

"Giving a massage to one's mother-in-law and putting up one's own hair are hardly the same thing," I snapped back, "are they?"

"You wouldn't begrudge your own mother a massage!"

"My mother doesn't suffer aches and pains."

"What if she did?"

"She would take an aspirin and lie down."

"Aspirin and a nap are not the only answers to the problem."

It was clear Haroon had spoken the last word on the matter, and so I bit my lip. Months before, I would have contradicted him. How well I now knew that medicines were not the panacea for every physical discomfort! Wasn't it true that the pills he had given me had not stopped my vomiting?

With Rosuni massaging Amma, Sakhina doing the laundry, and Ranu chopping the cauliflower, the cooking was left to me. Ranu was the younger *bou* and she knew very well that I as the elder had greater responsibility, and though Dolon swanned into the kitchen every few minutes, as Haroon's sister and the mother of the first grandchild, she had no domestic duties whatsoever. If the baby cried, she'd announce, "Somaiya is hungry," and come running to me and I would hasten the cooking. When I had supper underway, I went back to Abba's room to offer him a cup of tea before supper and inquire about Amma's aches and pains. Had the massage helped? No, she was still in pain.

When it was time to eat, I summoned Haroon's brothers from the television room where they were watching a Bollywood film; Ranu was fiercely crocheting in a corner of the room. "Lunch is ready," I announced, wondering how my sister *bou* found so much of interest in needlework.

"What have you prepared today, *bhabi*?" asked Habib.

"Lamb curry, cauliflower, and *daal*. Will that do?"

"Of course!"

I laid the table for lunch. The women—Amma, Dolon, Ranu, and myself—could sit to eat only after the menfolk were finished, and Rosuni and Sakhina had to be satisfied with leftovers.

In the late afteroon I stood at the window. As usual, I was waiting for someone without knowing who. Haroon never got home until late evening. I could feel my hopeful imagination take over. My handsome husband would suddenly appear, catching me after a shower, my wet hair wreathed in a towel, and hold me until I melted into his arms. "You're so soft and fragrant," he would cry, hardly able to keep his hands from my breasts. He wouldn't allow me out of his sight. I remembered now the day he pulled me naked under the bath tap, stroking me until my body became taut under the force of the water, making love to me as if we were beneath a waterfall.

But I would be disappointed tonight as I was every night. My husband had a routine—he'd arrive home, chat with his family, eat the food I served him, watch television, and then fall into bed. His body would meet mine only perfunctorily. Was this what happened to married people? I wanted to call Shipra and ask her if Dipu slept with his back to her as Haroon did to me. But Haroon disapproved of my keeping up with my friends. "This is your in-laws' place," he'd say when Shipra or Chandana called during those first weeks of marriage, and then one day he had our number changed. When I asked why, he said he didn't want to be hassled by job seekers, but I knew it was really his not so subtle way of letting me know he wanted me to keep away from my former life.

My reverie was broken when Haroon arrived home in a flurry.

"I have to leave immediately," he said. "I'm invited to a wedding."

"Have you been invited alone?" I asked. He didn't answer, except to ask that I press his clothes.

"What kind of gift do you think I should take?" he asked, as I ironed his shirt.

"Flowers," I said.

"How can I take flowers when I'm invited to a wedding?"

"Take them a book," Amma suggested, suddenly bursting into the room.

"I'm thinking of dinnerware," Haroon said.

"Ah, but teacups and saucers would be so much less expensive," Dolon said, getting into the act.

I watched as Haroon doused himself with cologne and quickly departed. I was getting sick of my memories of our dreamy courtship, but they kept returning. This Haroon hated flowers, but the one that had courted me decorated his office with a bower of fresh blossoms. Who had he been trying to impress with his concert attendance? His recitations of poetry on the sultry riverbank? Or were these just clever ploys to trap a girl with looks and brains, a woman with enough independence to meet him when he said, "The Swiss Café at five sharp."

"Where's the Swiss Café?" I'd asked.

"You don't know where it is and you claim to be a girl from Dhaka?" he teased. The courting Haroon had assumed I got around alone; the married Haroon insisted that if I went out, I had to take Dolon or Habib along.

"Why can't I go out by myself? I know my way around this city."

"Where do you want to go?"

"To see my parents in Wari," I said.

"But why?"

"There's no reason . . . I want to go, that's all."

"Why do you want to go for no reason?" In a way, Haroon was right to question me. Why should I want to go to Wari for no reason in particular?

"You're a married woman. You ought not to be going home so often. They'll think you're unhappy here."

"No they won't," I replied.

"Well if you must go I'll send the car and Dolon or Amma will accompany you. Or if you wait till tonight, I'll drive you." I was ready and waiting when he returned from the office.

"Let's go," I said. "It's getting late."

"I'm so tired," he said. "Can't you wait until another time?"

"But you said you would like to—"

"I did but—Listen, is it so important for you to visit your parents? If you don't have a reason to see them, why travel so far?"

"Forget it," I said.

Haroon knew I wasn't happy abandoning my trip, but he didn't apologize or say anything at all to assuage my feelings. Besides, it wasn't that I really wanted to visit Wari, it was just that I resented sitting idle in this unfamiliar house.

The next morning, I tried a new tactic. Why, I asked him, had I bothered to collect university degrees just to spend my life at home twiddling my thumbs? "I worked hard to pass all those exams. Had I done all that just to learn how to run a household?" Haroon looked shocked.

"What do you want me to say?"

I told him I wanted a job, that I couldn't bear being idle, that I had to work. He was nearly speechless with astonishment.

"What kind of job are you thinking of?" he sputtered.

"Anything I can get."

"Such as—"

"You have so many people in your office. Surely you have a job for me."

"But why do you want to work?" he persisted. I told him I had studied in order to work and that it seemed a waste for an educated person to sit at home.

"Don't I bring home enough money?" he asked.

"Of course, darling," I replied. "That's not at all what I'm thinking of. I'm thinking only of my need to put my mind to something useful!" Now I was laughing. "After all, an idle mind is the devil's playground!"

At that Haroon took me into his arms and then took my chin in his hands. "But sweetheart, you are responsible for my parents and my brothers and sisters! They all depend on you!" He gave me a kiss on my forehead. "Your success lies in winning their hearts, don't you understand that? Don't you know how happy you make me when you look after my family?"

"I wouldn't give up being a *bou* even if I took a job," I said.

"But can't you see how short of time I am? We married in such a rush! And now I barely have the time I want to devote to you!" Stroking my hair as we lay in bed, Haroon continued to speak, his voice tight with emotion. "This house is yours! You must look after it and arrange everything so it runs smoothly. There's so much work here and you say you have nothing to do!"

I sighed and then Haroon sighed, and then he changed his tune. "Okay, if you are so eager to get out of the house, go shopping with Dolon! Take the car and buy anything you want. I'll leave money for you with Amma." He was trying to pacify me as if I were a child.

But I did go shopping with Dolon. I bought clothes and pots and pans. And that night when Haroon asked what I'd bought, I showed him. "Wonderful," he declared, beaming. "At last you've become family minded." I showed him the pajamas I'd bought for Abba, the sari I'd chosen for Amma, a sari I'd found for Ranu and a cute little dress for little Somaiya.

"And," said Haroon, pouting.

"And a fatua with embroidery for you."

"And—"

"And shirts for Hasan and Anis."

"And—"

"That's all."

Haroon kissed me on both cheeks. "You're an angel. No one can vie with me for the best wife!" I couldn't believe that the simple purchase of an embroidered shirt could alter my husband's mood.

"Who can say now," he declared happily, "that I've been tricked into marrying!"

"Has someone said that?"

"Of course not," he said, chuckling.

That night in bed, he got entirely carried away, but it seemed to me as if he was making love to his family. I felt erased rather than embraced by his tumble of kisses.

From that day on, Haroon filled up my hours, leaving a list of tasks in the house when he went to work. Not only was I cooking, I was supervising new upholstery for the parlor and new curtains for the bedrooms. I realized that my lot in life was to spend the rest of my days in service to his family. I was no longer Jhumur, Haroon's wife, but Habib, Hasan and Dolon's precious sister-in-law and *bou* to Amma and Abba. I couldn't imagine how I was going to have any life of my own, now that I was compelled to merge my own sorrow and happiness with theirs, drowning my separate self in a stream of household chatter.

Right after we married, Haroon had taken me shopping one day when I was feeling a bit insecure. He chose a beautiful rose and gold sari for me and said, "How can you be sad? How can you imagine that I don't love you?"

I'd put aside what I'd thought then, that the gift of a sari, a material thing, can hardly measure up to what the heart desires. Haroon gave saris to his mother and sister and to all the women servants. Was there no way in which he distinguished me from the others? Was I different because I went to bed with him? Perhaps not. Most men bed many women; some frequent houses of prostitution when dusk descends, choosing a new woman each visit. What does such a man feel when a woman whom he will never see again rises to his touch?

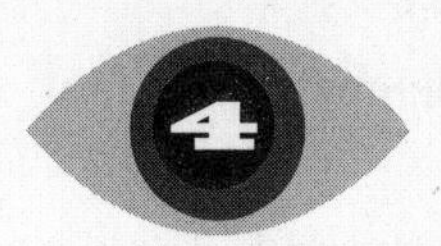

How can you have conceived in just six weeks?"

This was Haroon's new harangue, and he repeated it so often I became fraught with anxiety. What was wrong with me? If I wasn't pregnant, was I suffering from some dread disease? Though I was convinced I was with child, I was not given to counting days—I'd always been surprised when blood appeared on my underwear, and with the excitement of the wedding and the disorientation of moving into my husband's house, I could hardly be expected to keep track. But I had never experienced the nausea that now afflicted me every morning. Haroon watched me closely and finally one day, suddenly dragged me, ghost pale, to a doctor nearby.

I gulped down a cup of water as Haroon and I sat waiting outside Dr. Mazundar's examining room. Haroon was reading a magazine, and though I held one in my hands, I was too nervous to focus. When it was my turn to see the doctor, Haroon seemed reluctant to stop reading, as if he preferred we not consult Doctor Mazundar at all, as if the problem were all mine.

"What's going on?" the doctor asked.

"I vomit every morning," I replied. "I feel nauseated most of the time."

"When did you last have your period?"

"I can't remember."

"You can't remember! You look like a sophisticated woman."

"I prefer to be surprised," I said.

"Do you have any children?" she asked.

"No."

"We were married only six weeks ago," Haroon interjected.

"Have your blood and urine tested in the next room," the doctor said. "I'll call you after that."

The doctor soon sent for us, but before she could utter a word, Haroon said, "Give her something to stop her from throwing up!"

Doctor Mazundar laughed. "Of course I will," she said, then she laid me on the examining table in a curtained area of the office. "You're doing fine," she said afterward, when we sat, each in a chair in front to her desk. I felt a wave of relief and I could see that Haroon seemed heartened as well. Writing out a prescription, the doctor said, "I'll see you in three months."

"Why three months?" Haroon looked disturbed.

"There's nothing to worry about. Normally I examine a patient after an interval of three months. After that I'll need to see your wife once a month." Doctor Mazundar pushed the prescription toward Haroon. "Give her good food. She must eat well."

"I don't follow you," Haroon said.

The doctor laughed merrily "You're going to be a father," she said. "Go home and celebrate!"

I left the clinic, my eyes tearing with relief. I thanked Allah that I was pregnant and not suffering some mysterious malady as I had feared. I stepped out of the sunlight and into the car wrapped in a cloud of dreams. I looked at Haroon, but his face was grim. I knew in my heart that he was not playing a trick, as he had once when I told him it was my birthday, before we were married. He had not responded, and I was mystified, even hurt; then, as now, he'd kept his eyes on the road, a solemn expression on his face. But that day, before you could say "Jack Robinson," we arrived at the Sonargaon, a five star hotel, and he'd taken me by the hand into the dining room, thrust a huge bouquet of flowers at me, and, after a sumptuous feast, lit all twenty-four candles on the huge cake that a uniformed waiter wheeled to the table. After dinner, there was another surprise. When we reached my door, he presented me with a package, and an exquisite Kancheepuram sari fell from the wrapping, its molten gold embroidery flickering in the dark light.

I did not think Haroon was going to surprise me today. Even though we had news of our first child's arrival, I knew I could not expect another restaurant, another glorious present.

"Why are you so silent?" I asked as he drove. When he didn't reply, I looked at his sullen face. Was it possible he didn't want children? I'd been told it was normal for a man to resist having a child so soon after marriage. Men don't like being tied down—they want to remain unencumbered, to have fun, to go where they wished. But surely, if that were the case with Haroon, he would have been more careful or asked me to take birth control pills. I turned toward him once again, but his face remained stony and impassive.

In his silence, my eyes took in the road, the familiar streets—and I felt the extent to which my ties with the world were severed. Would I ever walk these streets again, run barefoot toward my parents' house, lose myself in play?

Haroon was still glum as we entered the house. He sat down and pulled at his hair, cupping his face in his hands. There was a look of deep distrust in his eyes but also sadness. I so wanted him to be happy! I sat down beside him, but he looked away. I took his hand, but he ignored the gesture. I asked him why he was so sad, but he kept silent. Then he got up, unlaced his shoes, and undressed, preparing to go to bed though it was still early. I didn't give up.

"Tell me what's bothering you! Why are you behaving this way?" Getting no response, I was silent. Because he refused dinner, I said I wasn't hungry when Amma called. A wife can't eat if her husband does not.

I resumed trying to mollify Haroon, running my fingers through his hair, stroking his face, asking him over and over again why he was so sad. Instead of answering, he jerked away in disgust, threw my hand off, and turned to the wall, his silence beating at me like a hammer. I still longed for Haroon to behave like Dipu had when he discovered Shipra was pregnant, dancing around with anticipation. Looking at Haroon, I felt sad and frightened, as if my heart were about to explode.

I couldn't bear it any longer. Leaving his bedside, I wandered to the window where I always sought refuge. It did not fail me, and I stayed there until well past midnight, staring into the night. Haroon did not call me to bed, but I knew that he wasn't sleeping, that all night he wouldn't sleep a wink.

As I packed his lunch the next morning, I asked Haroon again why he was so melancholy. He said nothing. "Why are you making me suffer like this?" I asked. Without a word, he put his tie on, as if no task required more effort than tying a Windsor knot. I couldn't stop asking myself if I'd done something to deserve this silent treatment, but I could think of nothing. How was it that Haroon was unhappy even though I was pregnant with his child? I went back to our room after he left, and I went to the bathroom and began to weep. Just as I emerged, wiping away my tears, Amma stepped into our room.

"Why has Haroon left without breakfast?" she asked.

"I cannot tell you, Amma. I tried to make him eat."

"And he wouldn't?"

"No."

"And you have no idea what's the matter with him?"

"I haven't a clue. I have asked him many times what's wrong, and he won't say a thing."

"Have you quarreled?"

"No," I answered feebly, my eyes focused on the ground.

"My boy is so good-natured! Just leave him alone, and he'll smile again," Amma said, closing the door behind her as she left the room.

I could hear her heavy steps in the hallway, but all I could do was hang my head. Amma had not asked whether I had eaten or if I was hurt by her son's behavior. Here she was, without knowing I was pregnant, advising me how to keep her son happy. I mustn't do anything to annoy him. I must please him. My proper place was at his feet. If I did not please my husband, I could be subjected to the serpent's sting, forced to swallow bile, burned in the fires of hell.

I remained in the kitchen the whole morning. Rosuni cut the vegetables and Sakhina scrubbed the pots and pans. At lunch Amma looked at my plate and sighed. "Poor Haroon, he must be starving!" I pushed my plate away and got up, leaving my food untouched.

"I don't feel like eating," I lied. "I'll wait until your son comes home." A smile of satisfaction crossed Amma's face. The ground shifted under my feet; it was as if I stood at the edge of a deep abyss. Of course it would hardly have been comfortable trying to eat in her presence, given my belief that I was the root of all of her son's problems, and, by extension, all of hers. All that afternoon, to distract myself, I went about the household with increased dedication. I prepared tea for Abba and rubbed coconut oil into the parting of Amma's hair. As I drew her hair into a chignon, she told me stories of her youth, when the neighbors came crowding to catch a glimpse of her long luxurious hair, which fell to her knees in silky waves the color of obsidian.

Soon it was time for Haroon to come home. I reminded myself of Amma's injunction—to keep Haroon happy no matter what. She was undoubtedly wishing me well when she advised me to cook what he liked best, to dress and do my hair in a way that would remind him of the girl he married; and never, never to rebuff him in the bedroom. "It's not difficult, you know, for an intelligent woman like you to keep her husband happy!" she exclaimed.

I dressed myself in the Kancheepuram sari, the one Haroon had given me for my birthday before we were married. I tied my hair with golden ribbons, rouged my lips, and applied kohl to my eyes. Seeing me all dressed up, Ranu joked, "Going somewhere?"

"No."

"Why are you all dressed up then?"

"Just for fun," I said quickly. I couldn't bring myself to tell her I had dressed so that Haroon would be pleased with me. So that my husband would talk and eat. And take me into his arms. But later, when Habib asked, I was emboldened to tell a happy lie. "Haroon and I are going to the theater."

Honestly I was getting ready to entice my husband into joyfulness. I had been moping for the past weeks, sick with my pregnancy, hardly worth talking to. Perhaps if he saw me dressed beautifully, he would take my hand again and we would go out on the town. After all, this was the husband who had taken me to the Swiss, the same man who had pulled me toward the best sari shop in Dhaka when I would have been content to visit a bookstore. How poignant it was now to think of those afternoons on the riverbank when he listened as I sang Tagore. *Tonight, under the light of the full moon . . .*

"Where have you been?" Haroon barked when he stomped in from work.

"Nowhere."

"Why are you dressed up?" I felt sheepish. Now that he had spoken so harshly, how could I say that I wished to dazzle him with my beauty, to remind him that he had not been cheated in his choice of a wife. I said nothing as he began to change into the pyjama he always wore at home.

"Let's go somewhere!" I urged. "Like old times! Those were happy days!"

"Happy days!" Haroon said. He staggered back as if I'd struck him.

"We ought to be happy for the baby's sake," I said.

"Baby!" He turned his face away with a jerk.

Haroon left the room in a huff. I followed and found him stretched out on Amma's bed.

"Are you ill?" I asked him as Amma hovered nearby.

"Maybe," he said. Amma was immediately anxious. She ordered Dolon to sit near her brother, dispatched Ranu to fetch him a glass of water with fresh lime, and suggested firmly that I stroke his hand. But Haroon refused all attention. He didn't need any drink, he repeated, and he didn't want the women of the house fussing. He wanted to be left alone.

I left Amma's room and climbed slowly upstairs to our room and my window. My face was still made up and I was still wearing my Kancheepuram sari. Looking up, I considered how close to me the sky was. It was this blue strip of sky that was my confidante. What might that blueness say about my husband's mysterious condition? Had he fallen in love with someone else? Or was he thinking of Lipi, the girl he had once loved? Haroon always insisted that old romance was finished, but hadn't I seen love rekindle, bloom again from dried up roots like a dahlia in July? It had happened to my childhood playmate Arzu. He had been in love with a girl when he was very young and barely remembered her when a chance meeting revived his passion, causing him to abandon a current girlfriend for that old love.

Standing next to the open window, I was desolate. My husband's house where I lived with his family had turned into a place where my most reliable companion was the blue sky and a quiet bedroom.

But soon I heard Haroon shouting. I found him, still on his mother's bed, screaming at Dolon who had done no more than offer to massage his temples. "*Bouma*," Amma said, addressing me as daughter-in-law, "where did you disappear to? Will you please find out what's bothering him?" Again Haroon insisted there was nothing wrong and that he didn't want me around. In fact, he said, he'd be really relieved if I left the room and got busy doing something else. But I had already prepared dinner and all the rooms were swept clean. Even Rosuni and Sakhina had finished their chores; I could hear them through the window, chatting on Hasan's balcony above.

"Would you like to have tea?" I asked Haroon.

"No," he said.

"Go and get some," Amma said, and so I went to the

kitchen to prepare tea for everybody. As I entered the room with the tea tray, Haroon left, insisting again that he wanted nothing.

"What have you said to him, Bouma?" Amma said.

"I haven't said anything." My head was bare, and I felt awkward at seeming to disrespect Amma, but there was no way, holding the tray, that I could get the sari over my head without the tray capsizing.

"You must have. Otherwise why would he be so upset?"

"Perhaps something's wrong at the office," I mumbled.

"Abba has inquired and there's no problem," Amma said. "It's you he's not talking to." Her tone was definitive, and I could tell by their expressions that she and Dolon had come to the conclusion that I was the root of Haroon's unhappiness. I decided to try again, carrying the tea into our bedroom.

Haroon was prostrate on our bed. I put down the tray, sat next to him, and placed my hands gently on his shoulders, but no sooner had I touched him than he arched like a bow, repelled. Usually if Haroon didn't want tea in the afternoon, he preferred a kiss.

"What's the matter?" I said, but again, he turned his head away. I sipped. "The tea isn't bad!" I said lamely, not prompting the slightest response. "Why are you doing this to me?" I asked, putting the cup down. "How can you be upset now, when we have just had this wonderful news? What are you hiding from me?"

Haroon lay silent with his eyes shut. I had always handled his moods pretty well before we were married, but now

I felt as if I were speaking a language he'd never understood. Quietly I got up, and as I walked around the room, I uncovered my head.

"Haroon, my darling," I thought to myself, "out of love for you, I've worn the sari you've given me. I've put up my hair in the way you like and I've placed a dot on my forehead. Am I not the bride you took so eagerly that first time? I've colored my lips with the red that once made you go wild for a kiss. Can you not take me in your arms, brush your lips against my eyes, let your mouth travel down to where your child sleeps, tenderly caressing my belly so that you do not disturb its slumber? Who will our child resemble, you or me?"

I was back in the trance of love I'd felt for him when he was the bold young man on the riverbank. "If our child is a boy," I continued to myself, "he will inherit your beautiful eyes, your forehead, your fine nose. I'm deep in an ocean of happiness, but see, I've kept our thrilling news from everyone else. How I want you, Haroon. How I want you on my arm, radiant, as we announce the coming birth of our first child."

I said none of these things, but I sat down on the bed again and gave Haroon a vigorous shake. "Tell me, which of us will our child resemble?"

Not a word came from his lips and his eyes remained closed.

"You know how discreet I am. I haven't told anyone the news, not even my family."

Then he opened his eyes. Not being able to read meaning into his sudden presence, I whispered, smiling shyly, "Look, you must tell me who it will look like! Look," I said, pouting like a little girl, "I know you want a boy, but a girl would be just as nice, wouldn't it? I'll name her Bhalibassa, in celebration of the spirit of our marriage, a name that means love. What do you think?"

Haroon looked at me, bewildered. "Are you not in the least eager to make an announcement? Don't give them a shock," I pleaded. "You must at least tell your mother." I leaned into him, bringing my lips close to his. This was what he always wanted, but he did not respond. His eyes remained cold, fixed as stone until at last he spoke.

"So who do you think it will look like?" he asked.

"You, of course," I said, running my fingers through his hair, laughing, bending over his body as I outlined his features with a finger. "Your eyes, your lips, your nose."

Haroon pushed my hand away. "I'll take you to the doctor tomorrow."

"Why tomorrow?"

"You can ask why when we get there."

"Not Dr. Mazundar—she said I should come back in three months."

Haroon scrambled out of bed. "To abort the baby."

"What are you talking about?"

"Just what I said. We have to get rid of this child."

"What are you saying?"

"I'm telling you what needs to be done."

My body began to tremble. "But why?" I asked. The trembling was uncontrollable. My hands and face turned numb as the room swayed and I clutched at the mattress to steady myself. I began to weep out loud. Haroon stepped back when I began to wail, but he didn't try to comfort me. I grabbed him with all my might. "This is our first child!" I was shouting now, tears bursting from my eyes. "It's our first child and you want to get rid of it? What's come over you? Who has put these evil thoughts into your mind? Who has come into your life that you want our child out of the way?"

"So you think it's possible to conceive in six weeks time," Haroon snorted, standing there, looking down at me.

"What are you talking about?"

"Just what I say."

"I don't understand!"

"Yes you do."

"But the doctor said I was with child. She didn't suggest anything abnormal. Don't you believe the doctor?"

"Of course I believe the doctor."

My mind was struggling to understand what on earth Haroon was suggesting. "Why are you suspicious?" I demanded.

"Because it's not possible for someone to get pregnant so soon."

"So you believe the doctor has made a mistake."

"No, she has not made a mistake."

"Then–"

"Then what?"

"Then why do I have to abort? Why?"

"You must surely know the reason."

"What's the reason?"

"Why are you pretending? You have asked me several times who I thought the baby would resemble while knowing that certainly it will not resemble me!"

"Why wouldn't it?"

"Because I am not the father."

"Then who on earth is the father?"

"Only you would know."

"You mean you do not know who fathered this child?"

"How would I know? How would I know whose baby you had in your womb when you entered this house! You were in such a hurry to get married! You gave me no time to think."

Hearing his words, my body went limp, the silken sari dropping from my shoulders, from my hips, pink and gold crumpling to the floor. I stumbled toward the bed to steady myself. Haroon thought I'd pushed him into marriage because I was pregnant! In one terrible moment, everything turned upside down—my home, my existence in my husband's family. A gale of agony swept away safety and certainly any joy I felt at the presence of the child in my womb.

Feelings of suspicion had been brewing in Haroon since our first night together. I was a virgin, but I had not bled. I remembered now Haroon fussing over the sheets to find a stain as I took in the pain of my first lovemaking.

Now, he was looking at me strangely. "You were lying then, weren't you," he said, "taking those painkillers to make a show of your virginity!" As I listened to him, I almost doubted myself. In the months of our courtship, he had come to know all my friends. Often, on the spur of the moment, my friends and I would come to his office and he'd take the afternoon off to drive us far into the Garo hills. They all adored him. "What a gentleman!" they'd exclaim, and I'd turn to him and say, "What do I need a gentleman for! I have a man to love." My friends had already decided I'd be happy with Haroon. "Ah, you are lucky," Nadira often gushed. "I wish I had a man like Haroon!"

But this group of friends was a gang of both boys and girls, and Haroon had seen how freely we went around town. I now understood that he was thinking I had made love with Subhash or Arzu, and that, pregnant by one of them, I'd pushed him to marry me, a rich man and a better catch than either of them. I could see it burning like an ember in his stony eyes, feel it as his gaze pierced my body, burrowing into my womb where he was certain Subhash or Arzu had planted his seed, where he could almost see a fetus gaining human shape, a nose that resembled the nose of Subhash, a brow that mimicked Arzu's brow. Seeing myself as Haroon saw me, I almost believed I was a degraded woman, a wily slut who had betrayed her husband, manipulating him into marriage. I felt a wave of disgust at what his jealousy had provoked in my imagination.

Suddenly I was terrified I had actually slept with Subhash or Arzu. Locking myself in the bathroom, I saw in the mirror a face that was not my own. In the light of Haroon's insistence, I saw a low despicable creature who had played a secret game of love with someone other than her husband, who had taken her place on the wedding piri not as a virgin but as a woman pregnant with a child not her husband's. I began to feel sorry for Haroon and to loathe Subhash and Arzu, dear friends suddenly turned secret lovers. I persuaded myself that at any moment Subhash would scale the garden wall, that Arzu would appear and rape me in the corridor leading to the front parlor. I could feel the heat of mortification rise to my face.

Yet, in spite of this power Haroon held over me, or perhaps because of it, I loved him and him alone. It was from Haroon that I' d learned the lessons of love on our wedding night, not from some errant lover. But now, because he had lost faith in me, I was too frightened to declare the extent of my love and desire, to tell Haroon that I'd married him quickly not to legitimize a pregnancy but because of a pledge I'd made to my father. How much I wanted my husband to understand that even now, in spite of all the misunderstanding of our first weeks together, it was him I desired and loved, for him that I forced my reluctant body out of bed in order to cook for his family, for him and a dream of our future that I chatted with Hasan, Habib, and Dolon whether I liked it or not, for the vision of happiness born in our marriage bed that I kept my head covered for his parents and stood in silence for their guests.

Once, before we were married, Haroon had taken me to the house of a business colleague who was away in Dhaka. As we entered the empty foyer, he took me into his arms. "There's no one here to disturb us," he said.

"So?"

"I'll make lots of love to you!"

"Now?"

"I'll love you completely."

"I don't understand."

"I mean I'll love you entirely, bring our love to culmination."

"But I have to go now. I have to be home."

I thought Haroon had immediately understood that I had no desire to be a mere peccadillo. "Do you take me for a moron?" he said. "I would never seduce you without your consent." He lit a cigarette and gave me a mysterious smile, resting his hands on my shoulders. "We can postpone all of this until after the wedding. I was just testing you."

"Testing me?" He was no longer smiling enigmatically and he had a satisfied grin on his face.

"I know now for sure that you are a good girl, a woman of virtue," he said. His words made me uncomfortable. I saw no distinction between girls who slept with boys and girls who did not. Why was it that girls were to blame when it took two to play the game? Hadn't Shipra and Dipu had a sexual relationship before they married? Weren't she and Dipu both responsible? When Haroon was madly caressing me in that empty house, I felt the heat of my body rise. I had wanted him to touch me all over, and if I hadn't been so hard pressed to get home early, I might not have rebuffed him. What could be wrong with two young bodies coming together?

Haroon hadn't let me leave quite as soon as I would have liked. "What's the hurry," he'd said.

"I have to take Kakima to the hospital," I replied.

"Who is Kakima?"

"Subhash's mother."

"Why you? Can't someone else do it?"

"There are others, but she wants me to do it."

"And so you go running instead of staying with me! Why can't you refuse her? Call and tell her you're busy."

Strictly speaking, Haroon was correct. Kakima could easily have asked someone else to take her to the hospital; the appointment was just a checkup. But she was family. She and Subhash and his brother Sujit had stayed at our place for almost two months when Subhash and I were at school. She loved me like a mother would, and Subhash and I often played at being twins (he was sixteen days older than me). The arrangement had come about when Subhash's father, Nitun, had decided to move to Calcutta and asked my father to buy his property. My father refused, but instead offered to help with money—he and Nitun were lifelong friends, and Baba was upset that Nitun was even thinking of leaving Wari, but Nitun insisted on the move and sold the property cheaply. There were farewells, but just on the verge of departure, Nitun developed chest pains. Very quickly, his heart weakened, and when he suddenly died, Baba advised Kakima against moving to Calcutta.

And so Kakima rented a place next to us and Baba became her protector and guardian to her children. Subhash and his family were not, therefore, merely neighbors. Though she did sewing to maintain herself and her sons, Kakima was always there when we needed her. She sent the boys to a good school in the city, but when it came time for Subhash to go to college she couldn't afford it. Baba paid the costs until Subhash got his MA and became the man of the house. I met Arzu though Subhash. They had become close friends in spite of the fact that Arzu was from a very rich family. None of this ever stood in the way of their friendship or of Subhash and me descending on Arzu's elegant

Gulshan house for an afternoon meal. Arzu was a playmate whose hair we pulled, whose back we thumped, and whom we teased to no end. Arzu and Subhash were my childhood friends, just like Nadira and Chandana, with whom I was free and easy.

Then I found myself in love with Haroon, a businessman. I hadn't intended to fall in love with someone who had money. Nor did I know the world from which Haroon came. I fell for his looks, his voice, and the way he spoke—the memory of it moves me even now that I understand it was not his everyday voice. He certainly no longer spoke to me that way once we were married, in that voice wet with feeling.

As I sat there in the bathroom, taking stock of the past few days, my mind throbbed with scattered, panicked thoughts. Everything was topsy-turvy. My life was being pulled down into a tornado, a gathering storm. I had managed pretty well, I'd always thought. But what I felt coming toward me was utterly unfamiliar, and I was too young to understand that my husband's irrational behavior had nothing to do with me, that he was in the grip of a monstrous obsession of which not even he was conscious. I had never felt such confusion and fear. What was I to do now?

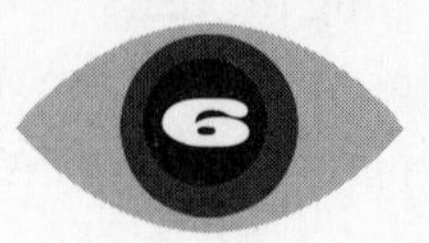

Haroon took me to the Dhanmundi clinic for the abortion. We'd told the family nothing and they thought we were out visiting friends. I had tried hard to talk to Haroon. "Look, it's our first baby, we can't do this . . . how can you be so wrong about your own flesh and blood? You're making a terrible mistake and you are humiliating me with these suspicions." I pleaded with him, reaching for his hands, but he jerked away, threw me off, pushed me toward the closet where my clothes were and told me to dress fast. I cried and cried, hanging onto the closet door. But Haroon pulled at me and said, "Change into fresh clothes, quick now!" I grabbed one of his hands and placed it on my belly. "This is your baby. You are killing your own child."

"I want to." Haroon's voice was harsh.

"But the baby is mine too. Have I no say in the matter? I won't go—I won't have it ripped from me," I cried out. But I knew I had no choice. I was, as Haroon said, his wife, and therefore contracted to do whatever he told me to do, no matter how cruel. I was at his feet begging, weeping. But he shrugged me off. "Stop making an exhibition of yourself!"

His choice of words did not surprise me. I had no doubt now that Haroon was unreachable. I finally dressed and followed him quietly, wiping my tears.

"Why do you want to abort?" the doctor asked before I was taken into the operating room. Why indeed? I looked to Haroon.

"It's highly inconvenient for us to have a child now."

"What's the problem?" the doctor asked. I could tell he believed that no man in his right mind would want to abort his wife's first pregnancy.

"We have no choice." Haroon said. He packed all his emotion into those few words. The doctor sighed.

"She's your wife?"

"Of course she's my wife," Haroon sputtered.

"Then why," the doctor continued, "do you want to abort the pregnancy?"

I was afraid Haroon would tell the doctor he wasn't the baby's father, but instead he smiled enigmatically.

It was as if I was shrouded in a fog of silence. All feeling in my sinews was suspended, my body like mist beneath skin and bones, as if I no longer existed but had escaped from the prison of the physical to some obscure realm beyond human reach.

I was not put under general anesthesia, and so I watched as the doctor scooped from my insides the gore which would in time have given way to my child's shape. The local anesthetic numbed me and I stared, dazed, at the spilling of the clotted blood, the vital fluid. If someone had found his way into my heart just then, he would have discovered a sticky lump of blood there too, but I could hear the doctor declaring the operation a success. "The womb has been thoroughly cleaned out. There is nothing left."

Haroon smiled, paid the doctor, and came to me. He sat next to me in the recovery room as I dozed. A couple of hours later, he drove me home. He announced to everybody that I had been ill, that I must be given hot milk, plenty of fluid. Members of the family took turns sitting next to my bed, giving me medicine or tea, even though Haroon assured them my illness was not serious, that I'd be well "in a matter of days." In the morning he kissed me lightly on the lips before he left for the office.

I hadn't been cared for this way for a long time, and, with relief, I came to the conclusion that Haroon was, in his own way, fond of me. Even so, I couldn't reconcile this new knowledge with what I had come to recognize as his deep mistrust of me. I couldn't fathom that he could imagine I would deceive him, pass off his child as someone else's! And if I was actually the cunning slut he imagined, why hadn't he turned me out of the house or dumped me onto the street with society's refuse? Then I remembered my mother once explaining to me how a man's desire differs from a woman's. "No matter how much you are loved," she said, "you are his possession, his territory." At the time I dismissed her as old-fashioned, but now her words returned and strangely, they comforted me. Suddenly it made sense that Haroon was giving me medicine rather than showing me the door. As the pain lessened, I saw the trouble he'd gone to—all the bottles of medicine arranged neatly in a row on my bedside table—and heard the concern in his voice as he reminded me over and over that I was not to miss a dose. I watched him closely. He was not smiling that mysterious smile anymore, though I saw traces on his face of the self-satisfied look he got when he talked about letting go a laborer at his factory whom he had caught in the act of secretly disposing of machine parts.

The family took my illness as being related to my stomach. Looking sad, Dolon remarked, "It's not good, *bhabi,* to be ill so much! Husbands get fed up." My sweet, innocent sister-in-law Dolon, pure as air, always laughing! She could say what she wanted, but if she did not take care of me, Haroon would get angry. And if I did not recover or if Ranu got sick, she and Amma would be without a *bou* and stuck with all the housework. Amma never stopped grumbling if Rosuni got sick—and Rosuni was forever panicked that she would displease her mistress and lose her job. Temporarily, I was free of those worries. Dolon could not push me to get up and get busy. My misery was a kind of triumph: there was not a single person in the household who could now punish me, hassle me or do away with me.

Little Ranu came to visit me. Sitting at my feet, she sighed. She suffered herself from abdominal pains, but did anyone rush to her bedside? And Rosuni! Sitting hour after hour on the cold floor, she declared that to get well, I need only brush a plantain leaf against my belly then destroy it by fire. I did my best to smile at the poignancy of her good intentions.

Even though the house where we lived belonged to Haroon, I thought of it as Amma and Abba's house. After all, they seemed to run things. "Your house," I would say to Amma. Haroon had no objection and Amma was only too pleased to crown herself with ownership. At the least provocation, she would go on about the authority her husband had once commanded.

It was Ranu who set me straight, "Whatever clout he had was in Noakhali where he was a clerk," she said.

"But Amma said he was a big officer!" Ranu made a face.

"A minister in the government is what she'll say next!"

Dolon came and stretched out by my side. She was full of talk about her daughter Somaiya, about how Amma and Abba wouldn't let go of her "for a second." They were mad about her, lost sleep if she spent even a day away. Dolon said she and Somaiya were living here because she was needed here, she said, to teach me, the new *bou*, how to run the household. "For the good of our family, I have left my heart behind," she sighed, but the minute she left the room, Ranu again set the story straight.

"That's all nonsense, her in-laws have turned her out of the house. Go there and see for yourself!"

How Ranu could gather so much information when she sat in a corner all day crocheting was beyond me. How she was able to discern everyone's hidden motives when she seemed to be paying no attention amazed me, but I certainly had no desire to become another Ranu. It's true that I had once wanted to get away from it all, but I began to see how much Haroon flourished in the heart of his family. I now understood that he would never choose a less traditional existence. And I could hardly believe it, but I could feel our love returning! And I accepted it despite what Haroon had made me do. It was better to live with love in the wilderness, I told myself, than to be lonely in paradise.

I was becoming well again, basking in my husband's love.

No one in the house knew that a child, our child, had been aborted, that our child had been taken from me in utmost secrecy. I still wept, but only to myself. Even Haroon, so close to me when we slept, was unaware. He'd started making love to me four days after the abortion, ignoring medical advice. I did not discourage him. How could I, still half believing myself a wanton woman? My husband had purified me, he believed, rid my womb of contamination. Chaste as a sacred virgin, I rose from the white sheets of our bed and walked feebly about the marital bedroom. I was a creature who sat in a kitchen that reeked of garlic, and, with Rosuni, cooked for her husband and her husband's family. A perfect *bou*, I prepared dishes to suit each of them, and, retiring at night, cloaked in wifely chastity, brought waves of pleasure to the husband who joined me between the sheets.

The doctor had advised that I take birth control pills for three months, so that my womb could heal from the abortion. Not knowing the truth, Dolon was appalled. "Why do that at your age!" When I invented an explanation, she would not listen.

"So you don't want a child?"

"Not quite yet," I said. I couldn't tell her that I was still in mourning for my lost child.

"But some women have three or four children at your age."

I went silent.

"Does Haroon know what you're doing?"

"He does."

"I'm surprised," Dolon said, pulling little Somaiya onto her lap. "Haroon loves children! In my hospital room, right after this one was born, he held her and made such a fuss that the doctors and nurses thought he and not Anis was the child's father." It did not surprise me that in no time, Dolon had told Amma I was taking the pill. Thereafter my mother-in-law spared no opportunity to remark that it was high time there was a baby in the house.

"I do not wish to die without a glimpse of my grandson!"

When his mother talked like this, Haroon listened quietly and smiled at me, and I would try to smile back.

But in spite of our returning love, I was haunted. In my dreams, a bloody knot of flesh leapt toward me as if to envelop me—not with shame but with red, vital fluid. In the days after the abortion, when Haroon sat by my side, I'd bled profusely. I wanted to go to Wari, I told him, to be with my parents. No, he said firmly. I wasn't going anywhere without the permission of the family. I belonged to them, to him, and they knew what was good for me. In my weakness, I understood with finality, that my future lay with Haroon and his kin and not in Wari. I was no longer a daughter but a daughter-in-law.

I found this turnabout in family relationships bewildering, although nearly every woman I knew, including my mother, had experienced it. I was mystified at the swiftness with which my near and dear had become distant, and those whom I hadn't known six months earlier were said to be the people closest to me. Marriage brought these changes, but did it also recast the mind, alter one's emotions? I was beginning to accept Haroon's family as mine, but I had not been able to erase memories of Wari. I longed for my mother, my father, and Nupur. By chance, one day soon after the abortion, Ma came to visit, bringing coconut pastries, mango chutney, and a luscious bunch of grapes. Amma sent Rosuni to serve her tea in the living room, and Dolon to entertain her. As I sat silent, Dolon chattered on about Somaiya—how the child liked to play, what she liked to eat, when she fell asleep, what time she got up, and what her favorite television programs were. Then Dolon had Somaiya recite a poem, and then another.

And so time passed, and I had no chance to embrace my mother or tell her about myself. How I wanted to confide in her! Especially about the abortion. But my dear Ma went away knowing nothing of my sadness, assuming my weakness was because I had a fever.

After she left, I stood at the living room window, which faced the backs of the houses on the street behind us. There was no garden there, just a few betel nut trees. Everyone had retired for an afternoon nap, and Rosuni was resting in the kitchen. But there, sitting on the balcony, was Dolon's husband Anis, the member of the household whom I knew least. I started to leave, but he stopped me. "*Bhabi*," he said, addressing me with a family endearment, "*Bhabi*, sit down."

I remained standing. "Are Dolon and Somaiya asleep?" I asked. I knew they were, but asking him the question was something to say. I had little to talk about with him, but I didn't want to be rude. If I said nothing or simply turned and left, he would regard it as an affront and, as the husband of Haroon's sister, he was an important member of the family. Amma, Abba, and even Haroon were constantly worried about Anis. The proper thing to do was to ask him about his business prospects.

"How's it going? Have you gotten the job you were promised by the Koreans?"

"That's gone bust—there's no job. But now I'm waiting for something to come up in Chittagong, thanks to your husband."

Anis was eager to find out when Haroon might give him an investment that would enable him to take a stake in a company. I hesitated to reply since I had no idea of Haroon's intentions, but I certainly didn't want Anis to know that Haroon never talked to me about business. I didn't like the idea that Anis, who was quite clever, would begin to have ideas about my marriage, so I remained silent, hoping he would assume Haroon took him seriously.

"Why do you look so abstracted all the time Jhumar *bhabi*?" His question jolted me into the present. No one in the house ever used my name; everyone called me just *bhabi*. Hearing my actual name gave me such a thrill! I have a name! I am a person! By calling me Jhumar *bhabi*, Anis brought me back to the woman I had been before my marriage—a university educated person with two degrees. I turned to look at him. Anis was tall, fair, and strongly built. The fine stubble on his round face suited him. I watched him run his hand down his bare chest, dense with black hair.

Now he was asking me why I wasn't looking for a job. "What's the use of a university degree if all you do is stay at home and cook?" A thin smile curled at the corners of his mouth, like the crescent moon that marks the end of Ramadan. Was he suggesting that if one cooked, one didn't read? Was he reminding me that Haroon had chosen me for my accomplishments? There was no doubt that a girl with a university degree had an advantage. Rosuni was an excellent cook, but Haroon would not have married her. My brother-in-law's question hit me like a torpedo. I could not answer him. I was surprised to hear my own sigh.

"Have you ever visited Cox's Bazaar?" He was talking about a resort near Chittagong, where the beach was known to be the longest natural stretch of white sand in the world.

"No," I said.

"Go there, the two of you! The sight of the sea will make you both happy."

"What makes you think I'm not happy?"

"I can see you are not happy."

"I am quite happy."

"You are depressed, Jhumar *bhabi*."

"Not at all."

"I've observed you closely, you know."

I felt a wave of shame. I thought I had hidden my pain. "You can go to the movies! Or to a concert! Why don't you go and spend a few days at Wari with your parents?" I laughed because laughing was the only way I could conceal my discomfort. Suddenly, I didn't care if I offended Anis, and I turned to leave. He didn't try to stop me.

I was amazed that Anis had seen my unhappiness, the drabness of my existence. The child would have filled my life with so many dreams! I had no dreams now; I was nothing but a two-legged creature living on earth to keep Haroon sexually satisfied. Anis had seen through to the heart.

I couldn't keep myself from anger. As time went on, Haroon would unwrap my sari to make love to me and exclaim, "We want a baby, don't we?" I would say to myself, "Yes, we do now, but we didn't then." I was still incredulous that Haroon had insisted, without any expert advice, that a woman could not become pregnant in six weeks. If I had reasoned with him that even one night of lovemaking could make a woman pregnant, could I have won the argument? But I hadn't even tried. Now he was eagerly awaiting the advent of "our child." He was so obsessed with the idea that he woke me several times a night to make love, somnolent bouts that were not about pleasure but which had the sole purpose of impregnating me.

In the days after the abortion, I had been so relieved that Haroon seemed to love me despite his suspicions that I opened myself to him, and when he turned to me after he was satisfied and asked about me, I wanted to seem the contented, eager wife. But my body was unresponsive; I couldn't give Haroon my love, and, in spite of myself, I began to hate him.

That night I asked him about investing in Anis's business. "That is a complicated affair. You would not understand!"

"Why not? Anis has told me about the business in Chittagong. You have taken the rest of your family into your confidence. Why can't you tell me? As your wife, shouldn't I be the first person to know?"

"What good would it do for you to know?"

"Do you think me so stupid that I wouldn't understand?"

"Who says you are stupid?" Haroon's eyes were glittering. "You are clever as a fox—or else you wouldn't have landed me in such a spot!"

"What have I done?"

"You rushed me into marrying you."

"You had no desire to marry me?"

"Of course I had. But not so soon."

"I was in love with you—I wanted to be with you!"

"Come on! Don't try to outwit me!"

"What are you talking about?"

Haroon calmed down. "The truth of the matter is that I love you and you only and I don't believe any man in the world would do for you what I do for you, but please, I beg of you, don't try to deceive me anymore."

And that's how it was. I wasn't allowed to go to see my parents lest I deceive Haroon. I was not allowed to step outside the house lest I deceive Haroon. His jealousy had built a cage around me, chalked out my limited existence. His jealousy was so deep he had destroyed his own child, but convinced himself he still loved me despite my "deceit."

Anis's suggestion that we take a few days at the sea had been excruciating. How could I enjoy the world when I saw it only from the corner of a balcony or through a car window? How could I, who was no longer allowed a glimpse of the open sky, remain truly alive?

A young couple rented the ground floor of our house, and the wife, who was a gynecologist, now often came to see me. I hadn't told her about the abortion, but she could tell I was not feeling well and brought me all kinds of remedies. As time went on, Sebati and I became friends and talked of many things, though, as good faithful wives, never about our personal lives. She and her husband, Anwar, who ran a nonprofit organization, had recently traveled to Sunderbans, to the tiger reserve there. Tigers are solitary animals, Sebati told me. A tiger moves alone rather than with a family as lions do. The female tiger and her mate come together during the mating season, but move apart when she produces a cub, otherwise there is danger the male may devour his child. Sebati could not know how sorry I felt for the tigress, how intimately I understood her loneliness.

Sebati worked at the medical college, and because Anwar so often traveled, she was free to come up to our place on days she wasn't on call at the hospital. Everyone in the family liked her, especially Amma, who carried on to her about all her aches and pains and about Abba's arthritis. The family was so grateful for her free medical advice that no one objected to the frequency of her visits. She wrote prescriptions for everyone in the house, and whenever she came to see us, Amma prepared tea and toast, serving her as if she were an honored guest, coddling her as if she were family.

One afternoon, as we drank tea in my room, Sebati looked at me and said, in a lowered voice. "Why aren't you having a baby, Jhumur?"

"I'm going to. Haroon cannot wait—"

Pulling closer, she asked, "Do you have sex regularly?"

I blushed and turned my face away. Sebati had no inhibitions. "Are you getting your period on time?" she asked.

"Of course."

"I get mine regularly too. Lets see who gets pregnant first! Listen," she said, her eyes glistening, "you must not miss having sex on the thirteenth day, even if you feel like abstaining on other days." I was still blushing, but Sebati went right on. She told me how Anwar came home to make love to her every afternoon following the tenth day of her cycle. "I rest during the remaining days," she said, giggling.

Sebati made even my most tedious days more endurable. A group of relatives from Noakhai came for a visit and I was formally introduced—all kinds of uncles and aunts of Haroon's. I had to keep my head covered, and touch their feet, which were filthy and wet with mud. And then Amma made me stand next to the window so that they could see in the light how fair my skin was. Lifting my head covering, she took my long braid in her hand and boasted of its thickness and sheen. I could see her mimic a sigh of relief as she declared how pleased she was that Haroon had brought home such a good-looking bride. She could rest in peace, she declared, now that she had such a perfect *bou* to run the household and do all the cooking!

"Bouma"—how deftly she tacked on the suffix that made "*bou*" an endearment!—"Bouma, will you pass the betel nut box!" As Amma chewed the *pahn*, she continued her list of praises. I belonged to a rich and educated family, she said as I passed *pahn* in silence. My father was a great university professor who had a house in Dhaka itself! We, his daughters, had all gone to college.

This speech was nothing new. Amma always praised me to the skies when people from outside the house were present. But when we were alone and I sat pulling gray strands from her thinning hair, she invariably complained that I had come to her house empty-handed. To marry me for love, Haroon had turned down such a rich proposal! The girl would have come with furniture, a new refrigerator, even a color television! And such a lot of gold they had promised—12 grams of it!

"But Amma, why didn't he marry her?"

"Haroon would marry no one but you. We couldn't do a thing about it!"

I knew part of what Amma was saying was true, but the rest of it was a lie. Our relationship was a big lie—I certainly could not trust her, but I now had a friend with whom I could be myself. I was so relieved whenever I heard Sebati's step on the stairs, I would embrace her, even cry, or we would laugh together until tears ran down our cheeks. How I loved to hear her talk of the big outside world! How bracing it was to have a friend who understood my entrapped life when so many things I had gained from my enlightened family were slipping from my grasp. My mother and father had exhorted their daughters to become educated, to stand on our own two feet. When I was growing up in their house, such ideas seemed to go without saying. What was there to strive for, I'd ask my father. Wasn't I on my own two feet already?

But now, these few years later, it seemed I was bent over on all fours. I was merely an animal; I had nothing to call my own. I had allowed others to undercut my well-being, and in order to have Haroon's unsatisfactory love, I had trained myself to be happy only when his family was happy, sad when they were sad.

And so, one day, when everyone was plunged into gloom at the news that one of Haroon's big deals had fallen through—a loss of one hundred thousand rupees—I too was plunged into despair, taking my place next to Haroon when he came home, pushing a plate of food toward him, and comforting him in a voice full of exquisite sympathy.

Haroon did not respond but sat there glum-faced, barely eating.

I tried again, putting a couple of pieces of tikka on his plate. "How did this happen?"

"You wouldn't understand."

In the days following, whenever Haroon came home, I could hear Dolon give a soft moan. It made me curious, but no one would fill me in. Amma was now always beside Haroon to console him, Ranu to bring him a cold drink. I was asked to do nothing. "Dolon has lost everything, poor girl," Amma sobbed one day. "Anis hasn't sent us any word since he left, so now Haroon must go after him to get back his money. After all, Dolon is his only sister." So it was an investment with Anis that Haroon had lost!

Amma was a very devout woman, and though I was well-versed in matters of religion, I was not as disciplined as she was, and now she was insisting that, for Haroon's sake, I do the *namaz* five times a day. When I protested I didn't know how, she flew at me. "You don't know how to read the Koran? How is that possible? What kind of woman are you?"

I looked at Haroon, hoping he would come to my rescue, get me off the hook. But he kept quiet and the next morning sent a messenger from the office with a little booklet of instruction on how to read the Koran. And so I began to perform the *namaz* five times a day.

"Pray to Allah," Amma directed, "that Haroon will be delivered from this mess." Good wife that I was, I became adept at praying to Allah for everyone's well-being and for my husband's health and wealth.

As for asking of Allah anything for myself, no one taught me how.

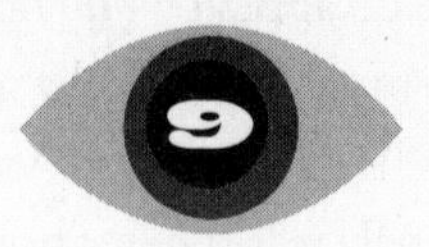

I saw him whenever I went out onto the balcony. Long-haired, sad-eyed, he sat in the garden below smoking or lying on the grass gazing up at the sky. Sometimes he had a paint brush in his hand and a canvas in front of him, sometimes not. Who was this beautiful man? I couldn't stop staring, and it seemed that whenever I was drawn to the balcony, which was soon every evening, he was drawn outdoors. Once it happened that our eyes met, and after that, we stared every evening. No matter how often Amma or Dolon called for me, I remained outside on the balcony, their voices hardly penetrating, so mesmerized was I by the languorous eyes of the man in the garden.

After a few days, I learned he was Sebati's brother-in-law, her husband Anwar's younger brother. "Afzal is a painter," Sebati announced. "He abandoned his studies to go to Bangalore to study art, and now that's what he does." I wanted to meet him, and one day managed to ask Amma if I could walk in the garden. She insisted I take Dolon and Somaiya with me.

Calling it a garden was a joke; it was more a swath of earth where Sebati had planted rosebushes and a few marigolds. We walked about, the three of us, staying longer than we intended, but Afzal was nowhere to be found. Why had he chosen this day to disappear? The bolted door of Sebati's flat made me feel empty. Heaven help me, I thought.

While Dolon chatted on about Anis's improving business affairs, about finally joining her husband, I daydreamed about those melancholy eyes. "Don't disturb the flowers, little girl!" It was a man's voice, Afzal's voice—Somaiya was on a spree, pulling petals from roses. I could feel his eyes on me, as Dolon picked up her little girl and headed for the house. "So soon?" I said. "Can't we stay a little longer?"

"It's nearly evening! Who knows what will happen if we remain in the garden with our hair loose. *Bhabi*, a stranger is staring at you, let's go . . . it's not nice." And so Dolon took the virtuous *bou* back home, unaware that my heart had already been pierced by the stranger's melancholy eyes.

I don't know who sets rules for the body or the mind. My husband was the only man with whom I had gone to bed—of course I had been attracted to others, but no one, including Haroon, had given me the kind of thrill I now felt. Had I fallen in love? Or was I, in my state of incarceration, attracted to someone as a promise of freedom? Or was it that, in close quarters for too long, I was claustrophobic and seeking relief in the attentions of a stranger?

My father had always told me to seek solace outside the family only if I was certain I could be totally secure. I wondered what he'd say if he knew the daughter he had raised to be as strong as a man had become merely an educated housewife, a clinging vine. But my father was no fool—he understood how the world worked, that a docile woman was what society endorsed.

When Dolon and I came into the house, Haroon was there. He produced two letters for me from my old friend Arzu. They were unsealed and I assumed Haroon had read them. I didn't ask why, and he didn't consider it necessary to explain. In the world I inhabited, it was normal for a husband to read his wife's letters, for a husband to decide if a letter was fit for his wife to read. Arzu had sent two copies of his letter, one to Haroon's office and another to me at home. Not much correspondence had come to me since I'd married—sometimes my parents called me on the telephone, but I never asked after my friends.

The letter had news of the death of Subhash's younger brother, and Arzu wanted to know how I was, whether I had forgotten my old friends entirely. He didn't give details of what had happened to Sujit, but he included news about our friends Nadira and Chandana, and how they all missed me when they got together for a movie or lunch. He was still working for his father's company, he reported, and our beloved Subhash was job hunting. My mother, he wrote, felt sad about me, though he didn't explain why. "I would love to come visit, but how can I when neither you nor Haroon has invited me!"

I read Arzu's letter over again to see if it in any way hinted that he and I had been lovers, even though we had never been more than friends. Haroon was standing right next to me, studying me to see, I suppose, if my expression changed, if a smile came to my lips, if my eyes brimmed with tears.

As I read, I kept myself impassive. I could see he was not pleased that my friends missed me or that my mother worried on my account. I folded the letter and put it in a drawer. "You've read the letter already," I said, "haven't you?"

"What do you care?" Haroon was frowning.

"I don't care."

"Then?"

"I'm grateful to have the letter. I wouldn't have known Sujit had died."

"And you wouldn't have known that Arzu was madly missing you!"

That last remark was something to add to the list of things I couldn't forgive. Haroon had made up his mind that I'd had affairs with Arzu and Subhash, and there was no way I could free his mind of that. And for my part, I was learning that even though my husband's behavior was governed by irrational beliefs fueled by jealousy, I had to take it seriously.

I was a prisoner in my own house, forbidden to step outside to see friends, and forbidden to seek a job, even though I was more than qualified. If I went out alone, Haroon would certainly accuse me of carrying on with someone else and allege, when I became pregnant again, that I was carrying another man's child. Under those circumstances, asking permission to wander the city on my own was not worth the cost. I was not willing to risk again submitting my body to the ruthless scraping of an abortionist's instrument. Would Haroon ever understand how wantonly he'd destroyed the truth and purity of our love? I could expect no such miracle. He was as jealous as Othello: without a shred of evidence I had been condemned. If I did not abide by the limitations Haroon now placed on me, I might find myself divorced, a condition no thinking woman would enter unless there was absolutely no alternative.

As my sense of powerlessness grew, my anger smoldered, and I could feel Haroon move away from me. I felt the distance between us grow, and at the same time I found myself thinking of the handsome artist in the garden more and more. One day, using the excuse that my shoulders hurt, I asked Amma to allow Sebati to examine them. "Certainly, *bhabi*. Ask her to come up!"

Sebati's flat was just down the stairs, but I could never get over the feeling that it was miles away. To be able to travel those twelve steps, I had to track Amma's moods, waiting for an opportune moment to make my move. When I got her permission, I went skipping down the steps like a ten-year-old, anticipating the moment I would be face-to-face with Afzal, as if meeting a lover I hadn't seen for years. I knocked at the door. "Is Sebati in?"

I knew Sebati was at the hospital and that she wouldn't be home until morning. Yet there I was, wrapped in my sari, veiled and bejewelled, the upstairs *bou*, unaccompanied. Afzal's long hair fell across his face, and his unbuttoned shirt revealed a bare chest, thick curls a pattern against pale skin. His black trousers were rolled up, just above his knees.

"She'll be here any minute," he responded. "Come in! Sit down."

He led me to one of four wicker chairs at the table in the center of the room, and I sat, supposedly to wait for Sebati.

How could Afzal not know that Sebati had night duty? Perhaps he did know. Perhaps we were engaged in a game.

The head covering slipped off my head and I let it, as Afzal sat facing me, watching me with intensity. I had never, even in my dreams, imagined that I would contemplate those moody black eyes from so close a vantage point. But now his eyes were merry, and a smile of pleasure played at the corners of his mouth.

"I have decided to call you Melancholia," he said.

I jumped, feeling as if a steaming fluid had emptied itself within my breast. My ears hummed with a sound that seemed deafening, but I calmed myself down, and ignoring his comment, said, "I see you love flowers. I see you in the garden very often."

Afzal laughed."You love flowers, too, I think," he said.

I didn't reply. Who doesn't love flowers! I had to have something to talk about, though I knew I didn't need to talk at all. I could sit as I was, enraptured in front of him, for days and nights, something I couldn't imagine ever doing with Haroon. Though it was foolish to compare Haroon to this stranger, I proceeded to do exactly that. I set Afzal's natural-looking stubbly cheeks against Haroon's blueish, clean-shaven ones. I compared Afzal's poetic eyes to Haroon's hawklike gaze. Afzal spoke in a deep voice, Haroon had a sort of bark.

"Do you have to sit so quietly?" Afzal suddenly said. "Why not talk?"

I laughed and so did he.

Then he told me how he'd left India sometime back and come to Dhaka on a whim with no intention of staying, but here he was, staying. What to expect of life, he had no idea—and so he was aimlessly drifting, but then again, he considered wandering superior by far to rotting in one place like a dead man on a burning bier. Anwar and Sebati had welcomed him, but now Anwar was pushing him to work.

"Don't you have a dream?" I asked.

"A dream?"

"Like earning money? Building a house and starting a family?" Afzal was laughing uproariously even before I finished the sentence. His laugh was nothing like Haroon's. I could feel myself quivering. It was a laugh that came from the heart.

"I dream of traveling and painting," he said.

"And so, it's a waste of time to marry?"

"Absolutely! Besides, who would want to marry me—a nobody?" he said, his mouth registering both complaint and the warning of another fit of laughter. A breeze blew a strand of his long black hair across his beautiful face. Such a contrast to Haroon! Afzal's clothes were spattered with color and his nose daubed with paint that I longed to wipe away with the long end of my sari.

"I'd like to travel," I said.

"Have you been outside the country?"

"No, never," I said.

"But elsewhere in Bangladesh?"

"I haven't stepped outside Dhaka," I said, laughing at his shock. "My husband can't find the time . . . " Now Afzal was laughing again.

"Oh, so your husband can't find the time, is that it?" I was embarrassed. "Then come along with me, my dear," he said, "India is half the world! When shall we leave?" He drew his chair closer. He was pushing the boundaries, yet I did not get up. Instead I played along.

"Why would you take me with you?" I asked. " What am I to you?"

"Well, why do you talk to me? I'm not your brother or cousin!"

"You're my dear friend's brother-in-law," I said.

"Absolutely correct," Afzal declared. "You'll tour India with your friend's brother-in-law!"

"Do we have to go that far away?"

"Are you afraid you'll fall in love with me?"

I was sure I was blushing. I was certainly biting my lip. I thought of Haroon. He had never relaxed and let himself go like this since our marriage. I thought again of those blissful afternoons on the riverbank when he'd laugh his heart out, or, the time in his office when he looked at me and said, "I wish you weren't so beautiful, Jhumur!" and I lowered my eyes and replied, "What nonsense! I have buck teeth and slits for eyes!" "You can't see your own beauty, but I can," Haroon had said softly. Now my husband offered no such lowered voice or dewy eyes.

"How can I fall in love with you without seeing your paintings?" I said to Afzal. He led the way to his small bedroom, where the paintings were stacked against the wall—now I was truly pushing the limits of my role as dutiful *bou*. An easel stood facing the window and on it was a canvas of a nude woman emerging from water.

Watching him look at his painting I could not help but think about Afzal as a sexual man. I took stock of his handsome frame, his full lips, desire rising in me. I wanted him to regard me with the same discerning look he was giving the woman he had painted. I wanted him to come to me.

"How I enjoy talking to you," I said.

"Why?" He sounded almost surly, which I could understand. But what he couldn't understand was that in spite of the fact that anything between us was impossible, I wanted him. He was smiling again. I moved to the window to stand beside him, and began to tell him about myself. I told him I'd had many friends once, but that now I had none. I told him that my life had become meaningless, that I was disgusted with myself, and lonely. My voice shook with fear, but also with desire. Fear of Haroon should he imagine for one moment where his wife was. Desire for the man who stood beside me. "Why this man?" I asked myself, as my voice turned thick and my fingers began to tremble.

I moved away from the window, the hot sun scalding my back, and sat down on the bed. Afzal took a seat in a rocking chair across the room and began to weave tales of his travels, of mountains he had climbed, of long walks near the ocean, of a stream he had followed down a mountain, losing himself deep in the woods.

I began to imagine I was with him in the places he described. That I had seen him leap down mountains and into the sea, seen him stand mesmerized by the sight of foam thrown up by the rush of waterfalls, turned silver in the moonlight; had watched him on a beach, paintbrush in hand, laying the colors of a sunset onto canvas. He showed me his paintings one by one: sun sinking into the darkness beyond a still river; a betel nut tree tossing in a storm; mountains turned black as evening rises and light retreats; a crimson slash of light emblazoned at the corners of a smoky sky; bronze reflections on the surface of a river; a dense flock of migrating birds.

"Do you like them?" he asked.

I could hardly answer. "They are beautiful," I replied.

"I've heard a lot about you from Sebati," Afzal finally said. But what had he heard—that I was a nice girl? A good *bou*? Was there anything else about me he might have heard? Not really. I was ordinary.

"So you have heard that I am nice? But why? Because I look after my in-laws, because I do all the cooking?"

Afzal's laughter in response infected me, and suddenly I was smiling too. I was behaving like the person who had gone to college and enjoyed being alive. I was talking and laughing again. We began to speak about the books we were reading, about music and poetry we loved. Afzal was like an old friend.

He admired Rembrandt and van Gogh, he told me, but also he aspired to paint like Monet, though he preferred women to water lilies and haystacks. He wanted to paint the nude female in changing light, to show how flesh took on one aspect in the morning, another in the afternoon, and still another when darkness fell.

"And so, is that what you are doing?" I asked.

"How can I?" he said, his laughter turning rueful. "What young woman would deign to make herself available to me for one whole day! What woman would make herself nude for the likes of me?"

I pointed to Sebati's cat, lying in a pool of sunlight on the floor. "Why must you paint only women? Why not paint that cat," I said, "lying in the afternoon sun?"

"Ah. I could never tame him!"

"What makes you think you can tame a woman? But if you marry," I added, "you won't be lacking for a woman!"

"I refuse to settle for a marriage arranged by my parents!"

"Then fall in love!" I said almost gaily.

"With whom?"

"You've roamed the streets of Dhaka. Don't tell me you haven't seen a woman you can love!"

"There are many women I can love, but they are all married. Wives and mothers—"

"Then who is the girl—the girl in your painting, emerging from the water?" I waited for the answer. Afzal sighed and did not reply. I was sure she was no one's wife, mother, or sister.

"Would you like some tea?" he asked, rising from his chair.

"Not really." Actually I was thirsty, but I didn't want to break the spell. I didn't want him to leave, even to go to the next room. I didn't want to suffer his absence, lose even a minute. There would be ample time for me to drown myself in cups of tea. I was gaining vitality every minute, as if breathing for the first time.

"I imagined her," Afzal said all of a sudden.

"Really?"

"Why yes," he said, turning his gaze dreamily toward the

window. He was thinking about that woman, no question. And I was certain she was no figment of his imagination. I could tell by her brow and the set of her eyes that she was from the south of India. Who knew where she was now, having retreated from the water into the fold of mountain and forest? Afzal's eyes returned from his dream and fixed on me.

"Your name is Jhumur, isn't it?"

No stranger had called me by my name since college. I thought of the days when Jhumur was my name and my sister and I danced, bells tied to our ankles.

"Your face is so beautiful," he said, "and I have seen you only in one light. How I would love to see you as the light changes. How I would like to look at you for an entire day." It was as if we were in a dense forest, as if I were hypnotized.

"Where did you find all those colors?" I asked, embarrassed.

And he too, chose not to respond directly. Instead, he said, "Jhumur, will you allow me to read your palm?" He moved to sit at my feet and took my hand. He pressed my palm, smiling, and my whole body shuddered. I closed my eyes and contemplated my ruin. I could hardly believe that Haroon wasn't watching through some chink in the blinds. I prayed that I could keep this moment secret forever.

Afzal, of course, had no intention of reading my palm. He spoke not of my future or my past but of his painting, telling me the story of his life as an artist, holding my hand as if we were old friends. Now the image of Haroon was growing hazy.

Then, abruptly, but fighting the desire to stay there forever, I pulled myself to my feet and covered my head again, obscuring my face. Quickly I crossed the room, unlatched the front door, and ran upstairs. I could imagine Amma's questions as I walked into the apartment: "What did you and Sebati chat about?" "What did she give you to eat?" Fortunately Haroon's aunts had arrived, saving me from constructing a lie. Sitting over tea with Amma, they were gossiping. "*Bhabi*," Amma said to me, "would you bring some more tea?" And, as I turned to do so, "Would you add a lot of ginger?" I could feel Aunt Sahedi's gaze at my back. She had once remarked that tea without ginger was like poison to her, which had made me laugh, and caused her to snap, "What on earth is funny about that?"

Now, in the kitchen, I chopped ginger root into bits and tossed it into the tea water. Looking out the kitchen window, I stared at the backs of the neighboring houses. Clothes were hung out to dry in the sun, a riot of colors—red, blue, and yellow—and I saw them as if Afzal had painted them. Still in the aura of his presence, I saw that red could be crimson or vermilion, yellow the color of butterfly wings or honey. Aunt Sahedi had on a purple sari, and her sister Kumud a deep green one, with a black blouse. I found myself musing that a white blouse would have looked better—a jasmine flower next to its leafy vine. Or that a red dot on her forehead would have emphasized the delicate red embroidery on the black blouse.

"Why are you taking so long?" Amma shouted from the parlor. I smiled to myself. The exemplary *bou* had thrown caution to the winds! Aunt Sahedi marched into the kitchen.

As I hurriedly poured the tea, I spilled some. She took the tray from my hands as she asked in a stage whisper, "What is wrong, my dear? Are you pregnant?"

"No," I replied, blushing. Pouring herself a cup of tea, she led me into the hallway.

"What's up?"

"What do you mean?"

"Don't you understand me, dear?"

Of course I knew what she was talking about, but I wanted to avoid the subject. I stood there, feigning dumbness, my head hung low. All I could think of was a cup of tea, but to ask for it would have seemed irreverent.

"Have a baby soon. A woman's life is meaningless without children." As I listened to Aunt Sahedi catalog the glories of motherhood, my gaze shifted from my toenails to her face and then out the window to the betel nut tree. Hard as it was, I focused my attention on her testimony about the agony she'd endured each time she'd given birth—and she had, bless Allah, five children! But she had known the pain of deprivation, at least vicariously. Her sister Kumud's condition she regarded with nothing but compassion. Her poor *bhabi* had produced two stillborns and was now too old to conceive.

"Many doctors have been consulted, my dear!" Sahedi said, heaving a sigh, "many specialists! I can't help thinking of how worthless her life has become!"

As I stood there, shifting from one foot to the other, Kumud came to my rescue, pulling me into the room I shared with Haroon. Sitting on the bed, she asked me to shut the door. "So many people about," she said. "I don't enjoy everyone's company." I fastened the door.

"What was my sister asking you?" she asked.

"Why I am not pregnant—"

"Do babies fall from skies? Have they ever?" Kumud assumed such a serious air that I could not help but be amused. She could see it on my face.

"You mustn't take what I say lightly. Come here," she said, "I'm serious." And so I moved to the bed and sat facing her. She dropped the pitch of her voice as if about to warn me of an impending disaster.

"Do you know what your uncle is up to?"

"My uncle?"

"He slept with Moyna last night as well as with me."

Aunt Kumud had already told me about her husband's philandering. Moyna was the girl who worked for them. I bent my head as if in sympathy for her shame and picked at my nails. I had nothing to add. It would not behoove me to express disapproval. Showing respect for one's elders was a tenet of faith in this family. Amma drummed that into my head day in and day out. She needn't have worried. In those ways I was obedient.

"Men are not to be trusted," Kumud continued. "They cannot be controlled. But I have done so much for him all of my life!" She sighed deeply, but then, suddenly, she seemed clear-headed. "Does Haroon get out of bed during the night?"

"Perhaps. I don't always wake up."

"Where does Rosuni sleep?"

"In the corridor, and sometimes in the kitchen."

Kumud stood up and began to pace the floor. "I've told your Amma not to allow servant girls to sleep in easily accessible places; in fact I've told her not to engage young girls at all. Do you think she listens! She'll learn her lesson if something untoward takes place. If Rosuni suddenly comes up pregnant, she'll pull at her hair and say, 'Ah *bhabi*, you were right. But how can I help it? The damage is already done.'" Now Kumud looked me sternly in the eye. "Tell me, Jhumur, you're educated. You ought to know what's going on!"

I was in no mood to continue this conversation. My thoughts had flown to Afzal, and instead of thinking about Kumud's ranting, I was watching the play of light and shadow on her cheeks as she strode back and forth across the room. I watched her figure glow in brightness and then turn dim in the shade, and I longed to be able to pluck the light from the sky and dress myself in its radiance.

"Are you a light sleeper?" she asked me.

"Not really . . . "

Kumud muttered that she was not either, that even the sound of a bomb exploding wouldn't wake her up. "Women who sleep soundly are in for trouble," she declared. "On the other hand, those who wake at the buzz of a mosquito or a breeze outdoors are gifted! Such women can rise at once and catch an adulterous husband red-handed!"

At that moment, I sympathized with Kumud's husband! Anything to be free of this woman's grasp, of her devilish harangue. "But Auntie, my husband's a good man!"

"Are you saying that your uncle, my beloved husband, is wicked?"

"I'm not saying anything of the sort. I'm just saying that Haroon loves me and that he wouldn't do such a thing."

"Really?"

"Yes. I'm sure he loves me."

"Are you saying that your uncle doesn't care for me?"

"Of course he does, but . . ."

"But what?"

"Oh Auntie, he wouldn't be sleeping with others if he . . ."

"Your uncle is extremely fond of me, you know. We don't have any children, yet he hasn't remarried, in spite of advice to the contrary from many of his friends. Do you understand?"

"Of course I do, Auntie."

"What do you understand?"

"That he loves you and that he has refused to take another wife—" I'd barely completed the sentence when Kumud shut me up.

"You talk too much, Jhumur. You run your elders down with your arguments. As a matter of fact, you know nothing at all. Men don't need love to have sex. They feel free to take as many women to bed as they want," she added, taking a deep breath.

"Just anyone?" I asked.

"Anyone they want. For example, if Haroon sleeps with Rosuni, it does not mean that he doesn't love you." Try as I might, I couldn't bring myself to imagine Haroon in bed with Rosuni.

"Haroon will go to Rosuni if you can't give him what she can, and, of course, my dear, she can't give him what you can.

He'll have both of you and be pleased as can be. Men like variety. Given the chance, a man will take as many women as he can, just for the taste."

Kumud was shuddering with rage at her own words, her eyes opening wide. If only Sahedi would come and rescue me! As Kumud continued ranting, I opened the door, pretending I had heard something, but she rushed toward me and barred the door.

"Where are you going? I haven't finished!" Her eyes were bright with pain and indignation.

"I want some tea, Auntie."

Outside the door Amma shouted for me. "What are you up to, Bouma? Why have you bolted the door?"

Opening the door a crack, Kumud confronted her sister, "*Bhabi*, don't you wish that I talk to your daughter-in-law? Jhumur may have gone to college, but she has no knowledge of what a woman's life is like. She'll face difficult times, I tell you!" With that, Amma pushed her way in and ushered Auntie Kumud from the room, back into the parlor. Now Rosuni was passing pastries. It had been decided the two sisters would stay for supper.

As the conversation shifted to what we would be eating, I turned to the balcony, hoping to catch a glimpse of Afzal in the garden. I could still feel his presence, his warmth traveling through my body, leading my imagination back to his painting, the mysterious nude woman. Did she exist and was he in love with her, or was she merely a creation of his imagination? Had they played together in the rain? I was surprised by my emotions; was this jealousy? I thought about the way he'd kept looking at me, a living, breathing woman, when his painting of another woman, naked, dominated the room. Did that woman have something that I didn't have? I wanted his gaze to turn to me, standing in front of him, disrobed. I felt as wet as the woman in the painting, just like her, in the moist darkness of my imagination.

I don't know what led me into the bathroom, what compelled me to stand naked under the shower, directing my gaze toward my own body, what brought forth the silver liquid that made its way through the folds of my skin, the tears that streamed down my cheeks. What had enjoined me to compare my own beauty to that of the painted woman, and what, by slow degrees, had allowed the woman to dissolve as I began to feel the force of my own desire, to bring my turmoil relief?

As the days passed, my friendship with Sebati deepened. Sitting around talking to her in her flat, I often exchanged glances with Afzal—we communicated quite well with our eyes. One day, I kept thinking, I would model for a painting. One day, he would paint my face changing as day passed and light fell to darkness. One day my body would adorn his walls, replacing my rival.

I came to feel as if I'd known Sebati all my life. I knew when she was at the hospital and when she was at home; I knew what she liked to eat, when she slept, or when she went out. We tasted each other's cooking. She came upstairs with fish curry, and I went below with a portion of whatever I prepared. We saw each other every day, exhausting ourselves telling our stories. We talked about our childhoods, our adolescences, and there was always more to tell. Sebati told me that as a child, she had always stayed inside, watching through the window as other children played, never wanting to join the game. "And now," she said, her eyes bright, "I'm never at home. But look at you! You were such a tomboy once, romping through rice fields—and now you spend all your days confined to the house!"

I wasn't sure if she felt sorry for me, her unfortunate friend. Maybe she did, and that's why she unfurled the spectacle of the wide world in front of my willing eyes, a world I had once relished but now believed I would never know again. In no time, she stopped calling me *bhabi* and addressed me as Jhumur, and I followed suit, calling her Sebati. Soon we even dropped the formal "you."

I became so used to her stories about her patients that I found myself anxiously asking after them. "How's Aisha?" "Have Rubina's stitches healed?" Her patients were becoming my new sisters. Aisha had given birth to a girl, her first baby, and her husband had stormed out of the hospital. Poor Aisha had cried the whole night, heartbroken and full of fear, holding the baby in her arms. Rubina had a tumor in her fallopian tubes, Fulera's uterus had become flaccid, and Jyotsana suffered from eclampsia and could give birth only to stillborns. Sebati's detailed descriptions of her patients' conditions began to invade my sleep. I dreamed a mass was growing in my belly, that my own fallopian tubes were twisted into knots.

But unlike me, at least so far, these young women were in danger of being cast out if their husbands came to suspect they were barren or could give birth only to girls. How would Aisha manage by herself? Sebati attended these abandoned girls with no less passion than she did a fertile mother giving birth to her third son. The health of every patient absorbed her. I couldn't get the young women out of my mind. What happened to the mothers of stillborns or girls when they got home to their families in disgrace? I could well imagine the slaps and kicks they would suffer, the dependency from which there was no respite.

I had a friend, Parul, whose husband had divorced her. To her parents, it mattered not at all that she had been tortured day and night by the husband who had released her, against her will, from their marriage. He had taken a new, younger wife, and they believed, that, of course, his infidelity was all Parul's fault. If she had given him what he wanted, he would never have subjected her to the disgrace of sudden divorce at the hands of a mullah. To make herself welcome in her parent's house, Parul was compelled to take the position of a servant. She aged overnight, doing all the housework, her mother never ceasing to remind her that no decent man would ever take a divorceé for a wife. Poor Parul—she had lived not two but three lives as a woman—daughter, wife, and now, the worst, divorceé.

In Sebati, I found a woman who didn't depend on her husband—a situation I had never seen before, even in my own home. Sebati's husband shared the housework, a rare arrangement. My friend Nadira's elder sister and her husband both had jobs in the bank, yet Nadira's sister was the one who disappeared into the kitchen the minute she got home, while her husband sat on the sofa and watched television. They earned the same salary and equally shared the household expenses, but it was always Nadira's sister who looked after the children and washed and cooked, in addition to holding down a job as demanding as her husband's. Sebati and Anwar's household ran according to a different set of rules. I couldn't believe my eyes one afternoon when I got to their flat and found Sebati sound asleep! When she got up, she explained that she simply had nothing left for housework after a night at the hospital. Anwar and she both lived in the house, didn't they? Why should she bear all the responsibility? Anwar had worked in Germany for two years and learned to cook for himself—he actually enjoyed it, he said.

Listening to Sebati, I wished Haroon and I had a place of our own so we could run a house together and share expenses and housework. Then I could take a job! I was certainly tired of cooking every day, of having to look after the entire family. I wanted time to relax; I loved the idea of sitting down to a dinner that Haroon had cooked, but when I told him about Anwar's culinary expertise, he sneered. "He must be gay." I wondered how it was that cooking took away one's heterosexuality. "Tell your friend's husband he should wear bangles on his wrists!"

Haroon was not aware of the extent of my intimacy with Sebati; he barely noticed when I stopped telling him about myself. In Sebati I now confided my discontent and loneliness, the distance I felt between Haroon and myself. She was sympathetic. Taking my hands in hers, she declared she would always stand by me. I might no longer have my parents and my wonderful friends, but I had Sebati, a friend whom the family tolerated. More than tolerated! They welcomed her because she was a doctor. Because she looked after them when they became ill. Because she wrote them prescriptions. Her importance grew exponentially overnight when Hasan was hit by a truck one day as he cycled to

Sarvar—both his legs were broken, and several ribs. In no time, Sebati arranged for a Sarvar colleague of hers to operate, sparing no effort to get Hasan the best possible treatment.

I visited Hasan in the hospital once, with Amma. There I found Ranu weeping copiously for her husband, sitting at his feet. She stayed at the hospital most of the time since Amma didn't think it proper for me, a *bou* of the house, to do hospital duty. "Stay at home and read the Koran so Hasan gets well," she said. I wanted Hasan to recover too! Didn't she think I would read the Koran and say my prayers without her direction? But I doubted just reading the Koran would help. Amma began to visit the hospital every day, carrying a thermos of hot soup and a tiffin box full of food. Dolon went with her—after all, Hasan was her little brother. Since Ranu was never at home either, the house was empty most of the time.

And so every night in my dreams I descended to the realm of my temptation. I knew that down the steps lay my desired object, concealed within a golden casket, as in a fairy tale. All I had to do was unfasten the latch. This was a secret I shared with no one, not even Sebati.

It was an afternoon when everyone was out—Baba had gone to Noakhai, Anis was in Chittagong, Haroon at the office, all the others at the hospital. Only Rosuni and I were in the house. After lunch, I found her stretched out on the floor, watching television. I was going down to see Sebati, I told her, even though I knew Sebati wouldn't be at home. Rosuni, of course, was delighted. My absence gave her freedom—she could do all the things forbidden her: sit on the sofa with her feet up, take a rest on any of the beds in the house, watch whatever she wanted on TV. She was, like anyone in her position, grateful for small blessings like snatching a few hours alone in an empty house.

The front door of Sebati's flat came ajar at the touch of my hand, and I tiptoed in to find Afzal sitting on the veranda reading a book, bare chested, wearing nothing but loose white pajama trousers. Quietly, I moved behind him, not wishing to disturb his concentration, engrossed as he was. And then, a breeze stirred in the room and the end of my sari fluttered. Startled, he looked up.

"Ah, who but the upstairs *bou*! How long have you been here?" I stood there awkwardly, saying something about wanting to see Sebati.

"I don't believe you for a second!" he declared.

"Why else would I be here?"

"You've come because she's out," he replied, smiling like a cat as I lowered my eyes and turned to leave. He took one of my hands, and as he drew me to him, I breathed in the warmth of his chest, not feeling the least inclined to pull away.

"Why do you wear so much jewelry?"

"Because I am the *bou*."

"So you do what they like?"

"It is expected."

"See if they expect this!" With that, he planted a kiss full on my mouth. Flabbergasted, I pulled slightly away, but he ignored my hesitation, lifted me in his arms and carried me straight into his bedroom. As I made a feeble attempt to withdraw, an image came to me of Dipu dancing in the clouds, and with that, I went weak, entwining my arms around Afzal's neck. As Afzal laid me on his bed, he was no longer Sebati's brother-in-law or the man downstairs. In our sweep across the room, my sari had loosened, and my hair had fallen from its pins. I kept my eyes closed—I was Shipra, bashful in her bridal chamber—but at the brush of Afzal's lips, my eyes opened like flowers, the woman on the wall coming into focus.

"What are you looking at," he asked, his hands stroking my cheeks.

"Your girl . . . "

"The woman in my painting? She was called Suranjana. I asked her never to leave me, but she did—for another man," he said, looking me straight in the eye.

"And then?"

"The man took off all her clothes . . . "

"And then?"

"And then he kissed her." Afzal was lifting my chin, kissing me.

"And then?"

"He made her run off with him—to a place far away."

"How far away?"

"So far away I'll never be able to reach her."

"And the place?"

"A place across seven seas and thirteen rivers."

We were hurling dreams like roses, swimming up through azure waves of some distant ocean.

I couldn't have placed what I was doing in my actual life at that moment even if I'd wanted to. Perhaps I wasn't there at all. Perhaps I had been incarnated into my beloved Shipra and it was she who was surrendering to these caresses. But it was my body that was coming to life, resounding with each stroke of this man's hands. How could I be enjoying pleasure with an utter stranger? Despite my romantic character, I was a traditional girl, a *bou*, and yet, here I was, throwing a lifetime of training to the winds. I had guarded my virginity in order to bestow a chaste body on my husband on my wedding night. I had never desired any man but Haroon. What was happening to me? Maybe this man and his bed, this man and his melancholy eyes and tender hands and taut body were a chimera, a delusion. Any moment Amma's voice would sound, bringing me back to the kitchen.

"Jhumur, why are you here?" I was startled by his sudden question, shaken. So this wasn't a dream. I was not Shipra, but Jhumur, the upstairs *bou*.

"I don't know," I said, my voice quavering.

"You don't, really?" he reached to take my chin in his hands, but I pulled back, suddenly frightened of what I was doing. I rolled over, placing my bare feet firmly on the floor.

"You said you wanted to paint me . . . " I said.

"I only paint nudes," Afzal answered, looking boldly at my body, my loosened clothes. My head was spinning. He sounded as if he were intoxicated.

I was not sure if it was my silence that encouraged him or whether he was a man always ready for a challenge. I didn't want to think at all as Afzal unfastened my blouse, caressing my body. My loosened hair fell from bondage onto his bare shoulders, my fingers played with his hair, his stubbled cheeks, his lips, the tangle of curls on his chest. He was watching the rise of my breasts. He was lavishing me with love.

The sudden sound of the telephone above us sent me, hair in disarray, pulling on my blouse, wrapping my sari, up the stairs. Rosuni opened the door, but she was alone in the apartment. I didn't speak to her, or ask who was on the phone. I headed straight to the bathroom, into the shower. As the water fell, the colors of Afzal's lovemaking, the sensuality of our bodies washed over my body with the water. But I would not emerge from this bath fresh and pure—my life had been shaken. Was I responsible? Or was Afzal? Perhaps our encounter had been a gift from the gods of passion, an exercise of their own pleasure. Impersonal. Pure. Tears soaked my pillow as I lay my head to rest. That night, when Haroon came to bed, I asked permission to go to Wari for a few days.

"Why do you want to go there?"

"Oh please . . . "

"Why go there? You clearly have no reason to . . . " His voice was brusque. "Hasan is ill in the hospital. Everyone in the family is worried sick and you want to go to Wari and enjoy yourself! I'm shocked how little you care for our family!"

I got up and went to the window. Soon I was weeping, but in silence. Haroon couldn't hear my tears, but I could hear him toss and turn. "Why are you standing there like an apparition?" I was no sooner back in bed than he began to make love to me. Now his voice changed to a tone of love. "My darling, please. I want a baby," he said, tenderness breaking his voice.

"And so that is why you won't let me go to see my parents. You want a son and you must have me every night." Abruptly, he pulled out of me.

"I won't allow you to sleep around with your old boyfriends! You are my wife! Have your parents come here!"

I said nothing, and soon he was asleep. As I lay there sleepless, any guilt I had about my dalliance with Afzal disappeared like receding clouds.

Hasan's hospital stay was eating up time and money and the life of the family. Every day, on the way back from the office, Haroon went to see him, and Amma, Dolon, and Ranu remained at the bedside. The house, therefore, was deserted virtually every afternoon, and, as for the flat downstairs, Sebati's maid and cook were gone by noon, and Anwar never got home before evening, and Sebati rarely did.

No one had an inkling of our affair—Haroon was not even aware that I had met Sebati's brother-in-law. As for picking up the odor of another man, he was so intent on getting me pregnant, he hardly paid attention to me when we made love. I tried to tell myself that I was involved with Afzal only to shake off the feeling of loneliness that had come with my marriage, but I couldn't help comparing my husband to my eager lover, and I was increasingly indifferent to Haroon's advances. One night I decided I wanted just to sleep.

"Get off," I said, pushing him away.

"Why?"

"I don't want it."

"Why?"

"I'm sleepy."

"Sleep later!"

"I'm not feeling well."

"What's wrong."

"I have a stomachache."

"I'll be gentle."

"No," I said flatly.

It was the first time I had ever refused him, and I felt a particular glee, even triumph. When he turned his back to go to sleep, a warning wound through my brain: "Don't dare touch me, Haroon. My body carries the signature of another man. Your bride is an adulterer. She has become what you have accused her of."

I was not without conflict, however. After several weeks, I found myself assailed by a flood of doubt. I grew pale, and would forget things, adding salt to the curry twice, letting the pilaf burn to cinders. Was I pregnant again? I tried to calm down, carrying on a dialogue with myself. I loved Haroon. I was the one who had wanted to marry him. But right after marriage, he had become cold and emotionally distant, and then he had forced me to abort our child. In my position as *bou*, I felt isolated and abandoned. Of course I was angry. Why was it then, that I had continued, until meeting Afzal, feeling desire for Haroon? It seemed just as mysterious that I had barely hesitated to break my marriage vows. On the other hand, I couldn't understand my feelings for Afzal. It couldn't be love, could it? Our lovemaking took place in some otherworldly dimension. I was wildly attracted to him, but love? Again and again I asked myself who I loved and again and again I found myself confused. Why was I not taking steps to leave Haroon and go off with Afzal?

An easy answer soon came to me. My instinct told me that Afzal couldn't be trusted. If he had come to me so easily, what would prevent him from going off with any woman who presented herself? Had I allowed myself to leap so quickly into an illicit relationship with Afzal because I knew somehow that I couldn't count on him? Though I'd had my suffering with Haroon, I was enough of a traditionalist to believe that marriage was for life. I couldn't bring myself to live with the disgrace of divorce, as Parul did. And we had been married such a short time. Surely things could get better. That being the case, why wasn't I content to wait things out with Haroon instead of turning to another man? For days, I struggled with my conscience, and at last the *bou* won out. I did love my husband, I decided. But there was something else nagging at me. I had to find release from the mental and emotional prison in which tradition had incarcerated me. Suddenly a shocking thought came into my mind. What if I became pregnant by Afzal, not by Haroon? My child would be the fruit of my independence.

In our conversations about our lives and the women she treated, Sebati and I had often discussed women's cycles and the times when they are most fertile. I decided that I would remain aloof from Haroon during those days. I would therefore not be offering him a body ready to conceive, but a fallow womb instead. It would be my pleasure to watch him wait foolishly, day after day, for his child to begin. As I thought about my plan, I had no guilt—I was not a loose woman, I was merely taking my revenge, getting even. Except for this deception, I followed all the rules of society. I took care of Haroon and his family, kept them happy and well-fed while living a desolate, friendless existence. I had the right to claim something in return.

A couple of days after I made this decision, my mother called and asked me to come home. My sister Nupur's daughter was having a birthday party, and Nupur would be in Wari for a week. I was unenthusiastic—I didn't want to be kept from Afzal. Hearing I was reluctant, Ma sent my father to Haroon's office to seek his permission. That very evening Haroon returned home. "Why not go? A week seems long, but why don't you go for the party at least?" I was silent.

"Have you suddenly lost your enthusiasm for Wari?" he asked. "You've been asking to go, and they want you so much. I'll come with you."

"Absolutely not."

Haroon assumed I was angry with Nupur and was pleased that I seemed to have cooled toward my family. It was what he had always wanted. And then, days later, Amma suggested I visit Auntie Kumud, and I asked Haroon if I should.

"Of course you must. Ma wants to take you along." And so I went over to Auntie Kumud's house, my head dutifully covered. My family, especially Nupur, were hurt and mystified that I had refused their invitation and assumed I had finally surrendered irreversibly to my in-laws. My friend Parul called to give me the news. My mother was weeping silently over it, she told me, and my father sat morose by the hour. Nupur was so agitated she had slapped her little girl.

"How did you get my phone number, Parul?"

"Nupur gave it to me."

"Did they ask you to call to tell me how they felt?"

"Not really—in fact Nupur was reluctant to give me your number. I had to beg for it."

"What did you say?"

"I said, oh, the poor dear! I haven't seen her for so long! She lives in Dhaka, yet I feel she's as far away as Mumbai! I just want to hear her voice."

"Do you think I'm unhappy?"

"Why should I think that? You married for love, didn't you? You must be happy, no?"

"I'm happy, wondrously happy, running my husband's house! Now we are looking forward to having a baby and we don't want to be away from each other for even one night! Besides, it's not proper to visit one's parents so often."

"You've hardly been here," Parul exclaimed. "How would being with your parents for one night interrupt your plans for pregnancy?"

"It would," I insisted. "If I see my mother's face, I'll produce a girl child. My mother had only girls—I mustn't risk anything so inauspicious. I want to give birth to a son, not daughters!"

"What are you saying Jhumur?"

"Have I said something wrong?"

"You're saying your mother is a bad omen. Who has a mother more loving than yours!" Parul's voice rang with amazement.

"What a heartrending speech! You live with your parents. Do you feel close to them? You slave day and night not knowing where you belong. You should be the last person to praise parents!"

That put an end to our conversation. I put the receiver down and splashed some water on my face. I wanted to be rid of all these demands. Parul would certainly report the conversation to Nupur, who would pass it on. I didn't care. I didn't want any friend or relative to seek me out. I didn't want anything to interrupt my becoming pregnant by Afzal. I didn't care if my parents were hurt or my sister agitated enough to strike her child.

Hasan was soon moved to a closer hospital. A piece of his fractured rib had pierced one of his lungs and another round of surgeries was required. Sebati arranged for a hospital transfer and for the operation and Amma and Haroon consulted with her day and night, inviting her to meals, buying her presents, including a beautiful sari. I was thrilled. One night, Amma declared Sebati an honorary daughter and asked her to be present at the hospital the day of the operation. Seeing Amma in such a benevolent mood, Sebati asked if I might be allowed to come down to her flat and help arrange her new furniture.

Amma was only too pleased to let me go and I ran downstairs, lighthearted. I assumed that Amma would tell Haroon where I was, should he call, and, as for herself, she didn't mind if I spent the entire night if Sebati wanted me to. They knew no one in the medical profession. She was their only hope.

Anwar was away for work and Afzal out at an embassy party—he was in search of fellowship possibilities for study abroad. Shifting one of the paintings to make room for a new table she had bought, Sebati exclaimed. "I have no idea what to do with Afzal! He paints only nudes! It embarrasses me in front of my friends."

It was a painting I hadn't seen before, and I was stunned when I got a look. Who was this new nude? A girl with long black hair down to her waist, eyes as dark as the depths of a pool, breasts round and firm, a blushing face. Could it be me? My throat went dry. I began to move things around to distract myself, deliberating where to put the table, a vase of flowers, the cane ottoman, potted plants. Sebati and I were deep in conversation. She was telling me that Anwar was incapable of giving her any sexual satisfaction and that she was paying a heavy price for marrying him. Her parents had wanted her to marry a doctor, but she had fallen for Anwar. Why refuse him? She discovered he was impotent on their wedding night, too late to change her mind. They had consulted psychiatrists, even sexologists, but nothing had succeeded.

"Sometimes I feel like leaving him, abandoning him and slipping into Afzal's bed," she burst out. I was totally taken aback. "Look at all the nudes he paints! I feel strange when I gaze at them, like stripping and standing naked in front of him myself. What would it be like to have his eyes rove my body? I want him to make love to me."

I tried to remain composed as I pulled my eyes away, and then, suddenly, Sebati fell upon me, weeping. Much as I wanted to put my arms around her and give her comfort, I couldn't.

"You must think I'm terrible for wanting to sleep with my own brother-in-law," she whimpered.

I wanted to assure her that I didn't think ill of her at all, but I could hardly make myself audible.

"You are such a wonderful friend," Sebati went on, her voice choked with feeling. "I can tell you anything . . . " And then she was suddenly upright and efficient, digging at her plants.

"Why don't you leave Anwar and marry Afzal?" I asked her.

"Who knows what's on his mind? Perhaps he's already in love with someone."

"Who would he be in love with?"

"I wish I knew." Sebati sighed. "So many times, when Anwar has been away, I have gone to Afzal's room wearing nothing but a flimsy nightgown. We've talked for hours, but he has never once looked at me. Instead, at a certain point, he'll say, '*Bhabi*, it's late, go to bed.'"

I could hardly keep breathing as she talked. She loved Anwar, and had compassion for him. Now they slept next to each other, like brother and sister. Time and time again, she told herself that she couldn't continue this way, but she hadn't found a solution.

One evening, soon after, Sebati made arrangements to sleep in a separate bedroom.

I had slept with Afzal for seven consecutive days, inventing a raft of increasingly imaginative excuses for not allowing Haroon even to touch me. I submitted to Haroon's sexual onslaught only during my period, giving myself to him as many times as he wanted, lying there, near dead. He knew little about women's cycles and was convinced that the first day of the period was a propitious time to get pregnant. He would not allow me even to go to the bathroom to wash—he was that serious about making me pregnant.

"Stay where you are," he'd say, frightened his semen would wash away even if I took a simple shower.

"Okay, my darling."

"And soon we'll have exciting news! As soon as sometime this month!" And then he gave me one of his gentlest smiles, hugging me and kissing me all over. Now I was his darling wife! "And this time, it will be *our* baby!" I still did not understand how he could have imagined I had cheated on him, bringing another man's child to our marriage and still claim he loved me, but somehow he had convinced himself the whole abortion episode was merely a mistake, that, like him, I was content to go on as before. Little did he know that in order to love him again, I had to betray him. How surprised he would be to learn that betrayal actually didn't come easily to me.

The next evening, fidgety and restless, I stood on the veranda, and when Afzal appeared, I smiled weakly, but when he motioned me to come downstairs, I pretended I didn't understand what he meant. Because I was sleeping with Haroon, I did not feel like giving myself to Afzal, even though it would have been easy. Rosuni had gone to visit an uncle, my father-in-law was in a deep sleep, exhausted from a trip to Noakhai, Haroon was at work, and the rest of the family was at the hospital. My lover was alone and waiting for me, but my mind and body were suddenly immune to him. I took out a book I'd already read twice and humming to myself, stretched out on my bed. But I soon dozed off, only to waken to the telephone. "Hello?" There was no response, only the sound of a deep sigh. I knew at once who it was and hung up. My heart began to thump. Was Afzal determined to be the cause of my ruin? I dialed Haroon.

"What's the matter?" he said, surprised.

"Nothing. When are you coming home?"

"Do you want something from the drugstore?"

"No, darling. I was just thinking of you. I see so little of you these days." Haroon went silent for a moment, and I wondered what he was thinking.

"Is everything all right at home?"

"Yes. Abba is asleep. I'm to wake him at ten to give him *kalojeera* rice and fish curry for supper."

"Has Dolon taken Somaiya with her to the hospital?"

"She has."

"I've told her so many times to leave the girl with you!"

"I know, but Dolon says she always makes a fuss about visiting Uncle Hasan. And she loves all the busyness of the hospital."

"So we'll have a doctor in the family!"

"Are you stopping there on your way home?"

"Why yes, darling," Haroon said, his voice thickening. "Tell me if I can bring you something!"

"Nothing, sweetheart."

"And you've become such an expert at reading the Koran!"

"I have indeed. And I prayed to Allah to make your brother well . . ."

"Pray for yourself, too."

"Why?"

"Ask Allah to give you a child!"

Our telephonic tête-á-tête ended with Haroon sending me a resounding kiss across the line. Putting the receiver down, I smiled to myself. Yes, Haroon, flood me with your sap . . . let your sperm run riot in my womb in a mad search for a fertile ovum. It won't find one, and you, Haroon, will never know!

I didn't know quite how much money Haroon had been spending on Hasan's illness. I'd seen him give his parents household money every few days, but he never discussed money matters with me. Sebati paid the downstairs rent straight to Amma. Maybe he thought I wasn't competent to handle our financial affairs. Such a contrast to the first days of our marriage when he went through his business files, identifying columns of figures as I sat next to him. Did he think marriage had slowed my wits! It was true I had hardly any interest in the subject, yet I'd now started to feel the need for my own money. I didn't have a penny for myself, but, of course, what need had a simple *bou* for cash? Haroon purchased whatever he thought I needed—a couple of saris to wear around the house, a jar of Nivea cream, even the most personal things. If I asked him for something he didn't have time to buy, he sent Dolon. He denied me nothing yet gave me nothing.

During the time when I had my period, Haroon took a day off from work; he had arranged a feast with three religious teachers who were visiting us. The feast was to take place in the evening, and Haroon kept himself busy reading the Koran, starting in the morning. There was a heavy smell of attar in the air, which reminded me of death. In the evening, I cooked for the celebratory supper while Haroon went out and bought a vast array of sweets from Allauddin's shop.

Dressed in formal attire, my father-in-law attended to the Moulavis, demanding tea for them and biscuits. Rosuni and Sakhina had their hands full, and I was working up a sweat running errands for Amma, who could not keep herself from complaining about her aches and pains. I arranged cushions and shawls, filled vases for the flowers and added sugar to the fruit ices, keeping my head covered no matter the awkwardness as I completed one task after another. Haroon strode about like the lord of the manor, pleased and satisfied that things were going so well and that he would soon welcome scores of neighbors and friends.

"Who should we ask from downstairs?" he asked. I was pressing limes for sorbet and a seed fell into the liquid.

"Damn it!" I spluttered, dipping for it with a spoon.

"Don't bother, you'll have to strain the sorbet anyway."

"Ah yes," I said, then replied to his question about our neighbors. "Sebati is not at home. She'll come up when she gets back from the hospital."

"Her husband is not at home?"

"Why don't you go down and see?"

"Has Sebati told her husband about today's festivities?"

"How would I know?" I was looking for the strainer.

"I believe she has a brother-in-law. We must ask him too."

"Do you mean her husband's brother?"

"Yes, Anwar's brother."

"Oh yes, Sebati mentioned he was visiting before going abroad," I said, pretending total indifference. Haroon promptly sent Habib down to Sebati's flat, but he came back almost immediately. The place was locked up, he said. Not a soul to be found. I heaved a sigh of relief.

Soon people arrived in throngs, the intensity of their cries of "Allah" resounding, shaking the house to its foundations. My body was also feeling reverberations. During prayers, men stand together in the open courtyard, while the women mumble their prayers huddled indoors, veiled and excluded. Because I was "polluted" with my period, I was exempt from any prayer at all. When the last guest had left, Haroon came to bed, eager to make love to me.

A few days later, both legs in casts, Hasan was back home. Ranu stopped her interminable sobbing, and Dolon left for Chittagong, taking Somaiya along. Sebati came to our flat almost every day, writing new prescriptions and changing Hasan's bandages. Amma complained all the more. She was feverish and called poor Sebati on the phone even during the day to prescribe remedies, which Sebati did, generously offering the free samples she received as a physician. Amma was ever more eager to please her. She worried constantly about what to offer Sebati to eat and took to praising her repeatedly.

I wondered, when she noted my friend's compassion and generosity, whether Amma wished Sebati were her daughter-in-law instead of me. A *bou* with a stethoscope around her neck is wonderful to imagine, but what if she were to set aside Amma's kitchen to run to the hospital to save the life of some poor woman? What if she went out before dawn or after she got home from her office to attend to patients at a private clinic? Would the family have tolerated her?

My period had ended, and I was ready to visit Afzal again. There were new excuses now to visit Sebati's flat. Hasan needed a new set of bandages. Sebati had left Amma's medication on the table downstairs for me to retrieve. But there were also people at home more often, and Afzal was even crazier for me now that I had less time.

"Jhumur, darling, where have you been? Have you forgotten me?" he asked when I stole a few hours to visit him downstairs.

"I haven't forgotten you even for a second," I told him. "I need you desperately, more now than ever."

He was eager to show the work he had done since we'd last seen each other. From a hiding place, he pulled out six paintings he'd done in a single day, one after the other.

"Who is that woman?"

"Can't you tell?"

"No," I said, giving him a naughty smile. He held a mirror up to my face. "Tell me you don't see your own beautiful face." I laughed, relieved to bury my face again in the curly tangle on his chest. When we made love, our bodies mingled in ecstasy as if to make up for my abstinence. Exhausted, I counted my blessings when it was time for me to return home.

"Going so soon?"

"I have to."

"You can't go now," he pleaded. I pinched his nose.

"You don't know what kind of husband I have! He'll kill you first, and then me. Don't make the mistake of coming after me, ever. Don't write, either, or call."

"But I am crazy for you. I've lost my mind."

"I'm not all there, either, Afzal, but you must understand that—"

"Come, let's go," he said, pulling my hands.

"Where to?"

"Somewhere far, far away. Australia? My sister lives there."

"But, my darling, I am tied to the family upstairs."

"Leave them."

"I can't. What would happen to Haroon?"

"Why are you thinking about him?"

"Who else is there to take care of him?"

"I don't understand, Jhumur. Don't you love me?"

"What do you think?"

"At times I think you do, but at other times I'm not so sure. Tell me, truly, do you love that old bugger husband of yours?"

"We married for love."

"I'm sure he can't make you happy. At least in bed."

"He couldn't earlier, but now—"

"Was that why you took a walk these last few days?" I giggled. "Why are you laughing? Why come to me if your husband satisfies you and you love him?" His face had turned pale.

"You wouldn't understand, " I said, kissing him tenderly on the tip of his nose. He stopped smiling and his brow gathered into a frown. I couldn't explain. I couldn't tell him that my attraction to him had morphed into something else, a dream of revenge. I couldn't explain that my infidelity to my husband was not about loving another man.

"I'll come tomorrow," I said.

"When?"

"I can't say. I'll come when I find time. Stay in, will you?" I smiled at him, and quickly left.

That night I told Haroon I had severe stomach cramps.

"What's going on with your insides? We must get you to a doctor. You're ill so much these days."

The next day I had a splitting headache. I swallowed five aspirin right in front of Haroon. "You're getting a migraine," he said.

"I think so too," I said in a feeble voice. The next day I got sick from eating food that had gone off and was feverish again the day after.

Afzal stayed in the flat throughout the week, and I saw to it that he did. After each visit, I'd seduce him with the promise of my next arrival. "You don't know how much I love you," he would say.

"How much?"

"So much that I can, with impunity, turn away advances made by other beautiful women."

"Really? I hardly believe that. You'll seduce the first woman to stand naked before you, whoever she is. You want me to go away with you, but what if you come across a beauty other than the upstairs *bou*, what then?"

Afzal's face took on a serious expression and he lit a cigar. Blowing smoke rings, he said, "Something terrible happened a few days ago."

"What?"

"Sebati came into my room in the middle of the night dressed only in a negligee. Then she took it off and lay down beside me, completely naked."

"What are you saying?" I sat upright.

"'Why are you here, Boudi,' is what I said. And she said, 'I've come to the end of my tether.'"

"Why do you think she said that?"

"I didn't ask. I didn't want to. I scolded her and sent her back to her bed. I can't stay here anymore. Anwar would commit suicide if he found out." Afzal was looking at me with those irresistible, wanton eyes.

"Why did Sebati come to you? You must have done something to encourage her!" I got dressed quickly and ran upstairs.

My breast bore the marks of Afzal's love bites, and try as I could, I couldn't prevent Haroon from noticing them. Throwing my sari aside, he rubbed his face against the marks.

"What's all this?"

"What do you mean?"

"All these red patches on your breasts."

"Love bites, I guess," I said, laughing loudly to take cover in sarcasm. Haroon laughed too. "No hope of that really!" I added. "It must have happened in my dreams when an old lover came and kissed me."

Haroon brushed his lips against the scratches. "Don't eat prawns for a while," he said. "They cause allergies."

I kept away from Sebati's place, and for Haroon I had stomach cramps, shoulder pains, or migraines.

It took only a month. Finally there were symptoms of a child. My period didn't come, and then my head was reeling and the vomiting commenced. This time I didn't have to complain to Haroon about my nausea. When he noticed the signs, he knew immediately what had happened, and from then on was forever embracing me, trembling with excitement, which, of course, was terribly uncomfortable.

"What's the matter with you?" I said one morning. "Why are you hanging on to me like this?"

"You're pregnant, you know."

"Don't be ridiculous," I protested disingenuously. "I must have eaten something."

"Have you menstruated this month?"

"I don't keep track of those things."

"You are such a baby! Don't you know how to count?" He was smiling, delight in his eyes.

I am just as calculating as you are, Haroon, I thought to myself. He was deeply in love with me again, holding me snug in the warmth of his ardor, forgetting, as he had before we were married, any obligation to family or business. I couldn't believe it. He exuded contentment, comfort, and happiness, but I could barely keep tears of grief from welling up in my eyes as I remembered his outrageous demand that we destroy our first child and the wasted months I'd been virtually imprisoned, a captive to his jealousy, separated from my family and friends. I had told myself that I loved him, but now, knowing I was pregnant, all my doubts returned. How could I forgive him? How had I been able to submit to his insults? And how could he be so unaware as to presume I might not exact revenge for the treatment I'd suffered at his hands?

He was utterly impervious to the fact that he had violated me. He had shattered my dreams and destroyed my belief in love, which was my only excuse for marrying into a situation in which all that my life and education had prepared me for was wasted! Instead of taking a job in a physics lab, I took care of my in-laws. I had dreamed of a happy married life that would not deprive me of individual freedom, that respected differences, allowed contradiction—a venture built on trust, sympathy, honesty, and compassion. How naïve I had been! How blinded by desire! How stupid not to have asked ahead of time what Haroon's dream of marriage was! Yet even in the midst of these thoughts, I was feeling a little bit sorry for him.

This time morning sickness brought a sense of triumph. Now, at last, I had achieved a modicum of power in my marriage. Because of my pregnancy, I was no longer the object of Haroon's anger and spite, and I had become pregnant on my own terms.

Haroon lost no time in sending a sample of my urine to the obstetrician, and two days later he arrived home with a huge bouquet of flowers. As he swirled me around the room, my thoughts were elsewhere. I remembered the misery of my first pregnancy, the days I had longed to be carried aloft in his arms. I watched his joy now. It could not be contained. He pranced and shouted, making such a ruckus that Amma rushed into our room to see what all the fuss was about. When Haroon gave her the news she touched her head, crying "Glory to Allah," a big smile spreading across her face.

"Lets have some pilaf and meat, Amma!" Haroon said, and my mother-in-law, no aching body now, raced immediately to the kitchen to make her special pilaf and curry, and, to judge from the fragrance that wafted from the direction of the kitchen, a cornucopia of other dishes. The next morning Haroon sent a message to the office that he wouldn't be in. "I cannot put my mind to a thing," he laughed, and dispatched Habib to the market for more flowers, to Allauddin's shop for a cake and masses of pastry, and then astonished everyone by kissing me in public. Suddenly everyone's gaze was upon me. By tea time, flowers filled our bedroom, and all afternoon relatives arrived in hordes to eat from a groaning board of sweets.

There was chatter to the effect that one shouldn't celebrate with sweets until after the child is born, but Haroon would not be constrained. He sent sweets to his office, to my parents, even to Nupur on Green Road. He fussed over me with one hand and with the other called friends and business associates with the news. Auntie Kumud rushed over.

"Haroon is really carrying things too far! Let the child be born first! What if she miscarries?"

In the middle of it all, Dolon arrived, but without Anis. He was busy at home, she said; he had rented a new office and his business was flourishing, so he couldn't be absent from work. Dolon was not here for the celebration of my pregnancy, but rather for Hasan, whose health still concerned her. But she would leave in a week—Anis had asked her to come back by then. "One mustn't stay away from home," she said.

"Indeed not," I replied.

"Anis is so clever, Jhumur *bhabi*. He couldn't run this business if he weren't! I have always said that no one can compare with him once he gets down to work!"

"So fortune is again smiling on you, Dolon."

"What are you saying? You must know how hard it is to be away from one's in-laws."

"I do," I said, but I could not forget what Ranu had told me about how Dolon's in-laws couldn't bear the sight of her.

Haroon put on a recording of Tagore, set to music, and then, suddenly, Kanika Mukhapdhya singing *My heart's desire has been fulfilled . . .* was blasting and he was holding me and kissing me all over. To please him, I lifted my voice in that ridiculous song.

"Ask your friend Sebati to dine tonight," he said.

"Why only Sebati? What about her husband?"

Haroon wanted Sebati to advise on my condition, but he invited both. I'd never before sat down to dine with Haroon, believe it or not. As tradition held, I'd wait for the men to finish before I ate. Now I would be sitting at the table, not only with Haroon but with another man! As we ate Amma's cooking and gossiped about Sebati's patients and Anwar's work, Haroon broke in with the news of my pregnancy. Sebati jumped from her chair. "Why have you hidden this from me?"

Haroon answered with a big smile. "We've only just had confirmation!—we're celebrating!"

"Do you want a boy or a girl?" Sebati asked him.

"I want a healthy child," he said. "It doesn't matter if it's a boy or a girl." Amma was serving us lamb curry.

"We'll accept whichever Allah gives us," she said. Sebati smiled.

"Does anyone want to know why at times X comes to match X and not Y? Probably no one. You know," she continued, "when I was little we played a game. Two girls would stand, hands joined above their heads, and recite a poem while twenty other girls filed past. The last stanza of the poem was. 'Here I bestow a pearl necklace on you,' and the girl who reached you at the end of the stanza would become your special friend, only because she'd filed by at just that moment. Whether your baby is a boy or a girl is just like that!"

Suddenly I felt sick and left the meat aside to have some fish. "Why are you eating fish when you are allergic?" Haroon asked, then turned to Anwar, "You had a brother, didn't you?" he asked.

"I still do," Anwar said. "He's not able to stay here though, so I'm sending him off to Australia to live with my sister. He's a good painter, and maybe he can make a name for himself there." My eyes met Sebati's as she quickly looked down and gulped a glass of water. It was strange that Sebati should feel so disconcerted at the mention of Afzal's name when it was I who should be brokenhearted.

I wondered what Afzal would think if he knew I was with child. Of course he would learn about it sooner or later, but what if he knew I was pregnant with his child? I comforted myself that he'd never know. Then my demons began. What if Afzal wrote an anonymous letter to Haroon telling him he'd had an affair with me? I swallowed some water, but fear stuck in my throat.

Afzal was an accomplished lover I told myself, and he was passionate, truly present. Only a man indifferent to love would write such a letter, would think to cause such havoc. Afzal had roused me from sadness and despair, he had kissed every inch of my skin, had held me, trembling, after every sexual act. I didn't know if that was love, but I was convinced that no matter how he felt, he would not want to ruin a woman he had held in his arms that way, whose image he had captured on canvas. Perhaps one day Afzal would fall in love with a blue-eyed blonde, and she, gazing at portraits of me, would question him, and he would say, "She was the upstairs daughter-in-law. I told her many times not to come and visit the downstairs youth . . ."

"And then?" the blue-eyed beauty would ask.

And Afzal would answer that the upstairs *bou* had long ago left home and met up with a youth who had stripped her naked . . .

"Where is she now?" the blonde would inquire.

"In a land across seven seas and thirteen rivers."

And I would remain forever alive in the landscape of his imagination, even though he might not remember my name, might even mistake another woman for me. I asked myself whether I regretted losing him, and came to the conclusion that I did not. Instead, I was glad that I would, perhaps, never see him again, except in my dreams. He had wanted me to run away with him. I could be nothing but relieved that he was going to Australia, I realized. Had I divorced and married him, he would not have made things easy for me. After all, what man could trust a woman who had come to him while still married to another man?

After dinner, Haroon took Anwar into the sitting room for an old-fashioned male conversation about politics and finance. Each taking *pahn* from Amma's betel box, Sebati and I went up to the bedroom. Chewing on the aromatic nut, we stretched out on the bed and talked about my coming child.

"You've won," Sebati exclaimed.

"And my reward from you?"

"Whatever you wish," she said, her eyes shining.

"That I never, ever, lose your friendship."

"Never, Jhumur. You will never lose me." And then she began to speak as a doctor, advising me not to sleep with Haroon during the first three months of pregnancy.

"Wonderful! But of course," I said laughing, "I may sleep with another man!"

"Absolutely!" she giggled. "I can say with considerable conviction that there is no harm in that!" And we both roared with laughter.

When we had calmed down, I took her hand.

"Tell me, is your brother-in-law really going away?"

Sebati sighed.

"To tell you the truth, I don't want him to stay on with us. It has become quite intolerable."

She lowered her voice. "You know that I sleep in another room these days. One night I was awakened by a sound, and there was Afzal at the foot of my bed without a shred of clothing. He lay down and began to pull at my sari. What more do I have to tell you? He wanted to sleep with me. I scolded him and sent him away." Sebati was shaking all over.

"But didn't you yourself tell me that you were very attracted to him?"

"Fantasizing and acting are not the same thing," she said. "In any case, I said all that because I was frustrated and angry at Anwar, but don't forget, I am, after all, Afzal's sister-in-law. And Anwar simply adores his little brother and would do anything for him. He's arranging this trip to Australia for him! Do you think that Afzal could possibly work that out on his own?"

Sebati's revelation left me at a loss for words. She went on. "I don't want him to stay. I really don't." I could see tears in her eyes. "Anwar has no idea and he'd become murderous if he knew. Anwar and I—we rely on each other. We are close friends even though we don't have sex. I treasure my relationship with him, and I wouldn't want to damage it in any way."

I had no idea which story, Afzal's or Sebati's, was the truth. I could not listen any longer and changed the subject.

"What should I take for morning sickness? " I asked her,

and she said she would bring me a pill that wouldn't harm the fetus, and also some iron tablets.

That night, in Haroon's arms, I thought about Sebati's situation. I felt such compassion for her. Then, in the dark, I stroked my own arm in the way Afzal had and tried to imagine him comforting Sebati, making her happy. How could she have refused him? Or had he refused her?

"Didn't I tell you not to eat hilsa fish? Your arms get all blotchy and then you scratch them." Haroon had burst into my reverie.

"Stop worrying," I said, scratching some more. Haroon placed his fingers gently on Afzal's love bites, now healing, but still slightly itchy. "A nice person, Anwar is," he said.

"What did he have to say," I asked.

"He said he loved children and wanted to become a father, but that Sebati wouldn't agree. Her heart is set on a post-graduate degree in medicine."

"Is that so?"

Whenever I was about to drop off to sleep, a faint sound of weeping would break the night silence. After Haroon dozed off, I tiptoed out and entered Dolon's room, to find her sobbing, her face against the pillow. Going to her, I placed my hand on her shoulder.

"Why are you crying?" I asked. She ceased sobbing but didn't reply at first, then she mumbled.

"I worry about Anis so much."

"But why?"

"He's all alone. He hates being without me. He won't eat anyone else's cooking and he doesn't sleep without me by his side."

"Ask him to come here or else go home to him," I said, stroking her gently. Dolon threw aside my hand and sat up.

"How can I go, *bhabi*? How can you even suggest that? Who will look after Hasan and Ranu? That slip of a girl does nothing. All she knows how to do is whine. How will Hasan ever recover with her as his wife?"

"But we are all taking care of Hasan—"

"No, no." Dolon was weeping again. She said Hasan himself had complained of being neglected. His lungs had to be drained repeatedly, his left leg was so numb that he doubted he'd ever be able to use it again. And he was sure the wound was infected.

I stayed with Dolon until she dozed off, and then I returned to my bed. It was late, but there was too much for me to absorb to think of sleeping, so I went to stand at the window. The strong smell of night-blooming jasmine wafted in from the garden. I breathed, allowing the scent to fill my nostrils and my lungs. I had always heard that snakes come out of their burrows, lured by that night fragrance. I felt like going outdoors and lying on the earth, close to the moist fragrance of those sweet smelling flowers.

Weeks passed and my abdomen grew heavy. Haroon decreed I was to do no more housework.

"But how will I pass the time?"

"You must rest a lot, eat plenty of vegetables, meat, and fruit."

"I can't eat that much food."

"It's for the child. It must be born healthy!"

Haroon brought all sorts of journals and newspapers home, and he placed a new television set in our bedroom. Now all I did was lie in bed all day and read and watch ridiculous TV shows. My room was fragrant with flowers, and I ate whatever Amma or Ranu cooked for me. Haroon now came home early; he got restless, he said. It was all he could do to stay at the office until noon. He arrived, laden with flowers and produce, fresh milk, fruit juice, the makings of hot chocolate. I could never consume all he brought, and so I passed it on to the family, and still there were always leftovers.

It shocked me how the precious burden in my womb altered my position in the household. Amma was forever running into my room to make sure I was well or to bring me something scrumptious to eat. She liked to be able to tell Haroon that she was taking special care of me. That was no surprise. Mothers are totally beholden to their sons and go to great lengths to keep them in good humor even while keeping their daughters-in-law under a reign of terror. Certainly in our household, Haroon—and his money—called the shots.

As it was, everyone in the family followed Amma's example, even good-for-nothing Habib. "*Bhabi*, do you want something? *Bhabi*, shall I fetch you a dish of cool sorbet?"

Poor Hasan, limping along on his crutches, came to pay his respects one day. For a while he sat by the window gazing soulfully at the sky, and then he burst out, "What's there to dream of!" He and Ranu wanted to move to Saudi Arabia—"The skies are so wide there," he'd told me one day, and I'd answered that it was not the sky that was different elsewhere, but other things. "Other things are insignificant to me," he'd said. "The sky is all that matters." Even though he had grown up in this very practical family, Hasan was a dreamer. He and Ranu got along well—secretly he brought her presents, oranges or a pretty compact. They actually seemed to be in love, a less complicated love than I felt toward Haroon.

How I relished the spectacle of Amma sewing tiny clothes for the soon to arrive infant, embroidering little jackets and hats. And the new Haroon who took me to the Dhanmundi clinic at intervals of a few days, warmly greeting Sebati, who was always there to guide us, even though she had a lot of work to do, and her post-graduate entrance exams were coming up.

When Haroon was at the office, I often chatted with Ranu. Unknotting my hair one day, she said, "You're educated—no wonder everyone in the house respects you so."

"Why do you say that? Do you feel overlooked?"

"That's not it," she said, pursing her lips.

"What then?"

"I have to cover myself whenever I go out, and you don't."

"You don't have to either if you don't want to," I said.

"Amma would never allow me out unveiled. Besides, my husband doesn't have a job. If he did, she would have nothing to say about whether I covered my head or not."

Then one day, Ranu came crying into my room. "The police have arrested Anis," she said.

"The police? Whatever for?"

"They have taken his two associates as well. Apparently they were involved in smuggling."

"What are you saying?" I was thunderstruck, remembering my conversations with Dolon about how well her husband was doing in business. "Is that the reason Anis is staying on in Chittagong?"

"Must be."

"Does Haroon know about this?"

"I'm sure he must." Ranu said.

"What about Dolon?" She was here visiting us again, but I knew she was hell-bent on getting back to Chittagong.

"*Bhabi*, you're so naive!" Ranu said. "Don't you know Dolon's father-in-law caught Anis with another woman the last time he was in Chittagong? It was Haroon who ordered Dolon straight back to Dhaka."

So that was the real reason Dolon wept at night. I was speechless. Haroon had kept all of this from me. Ranu went on. "We are so grateful to you, *bhabi*. Haroon is bearing all our expenses. He is a god! If I were in your place, I would never have allowed it. Doesn't it make you angry?"

"It's complicated," I replied, trying to sound indifferent.

"Don't you want to live in a place of your own? I do."

I laughed, taking her hand. I too had such dreams. A dream of life under an open sky. I have forgotten those dreams, I thought, forgotten even what a blue sky looks like!

Looking intently into my eyes, Ranu said, "Please, please ask Haroon to give him some money."

"Which him is that?"

"Don't you know? Him. My husband."

I started to laugh out loud. She couldn't speak Hasan's name because he was her husband! But I swallowed my laughter. Wasn't I bound by the same rules? I never uttered Haroon's name in public. What was the difference between Ranu and me, between Amma and me, between Dolon and me? We all lived under the same constraints!

"Please, please ask Haroon to set him up in some business."

"Why doesn't Hasan talk to Haroon directly?"

"He's too timid. He can hardly speak to anyone." Ranu sighed. "But Haroon should invest in Hasan! My husband is his own brother, and he has already given sixty thousand rupees to Anis, who is related to him only by marriage. My poor husband is so desolate, he can hardly get out of bed. *Bhabi*, please, please talk to Haroon!"

"Haroon is deeply concerned about his family. I'm sure I don't need to remind him."

"But he will listen to you. What you say carries weight. Oh *bhabi*, you have prestige in this house."

"It's not me. The prestige I suddenly have is because I'm with child, and the child to whom I give birth will carry on the family. My words don't matter. You and I are in the same situation, exactly. We are powerless."

"Then how can Dolon throw her weight around so recklessly?"

I shut my eyes. I was sleepy so much of the time now. Ranu came close and whispered. "Know why Dolon can't visit her in-laws? She hit her mother-in-law! She threw a dish at her! She's become a devil, if you ask me!"

I don't know when Ranu left, but late that afternoon, Sebati woke me up. She examined my eyes to see if I was anemic, felt my pulse, checked my blood pressure, tapped my lungs, and declared I was one hundred percent fit.

"Afzal is preparing to leave," she said.

"Really? When?"

"On the twenty-seventh of this month." She looked pale, as if she wanted to talk about Afzal, but I wouldn't let her.

"When are your exams?" I asked.

"Not for a while, but I'm working very hard. I never get to bed until almost dawn."

"Is Afzal still bothering you?"

"He wouldn't dare. He's such a wimp!" Sebati really did look haggard, as if she hadn't eaten for days. I wondered if she would have been so angry at Afzal if he had come to her rescue. And then she said, "At least he's stopped painting those female nudes!" I thought the paintings of me were safely hidden, but clearly Sebati didn't see me in her brother-in-law's studies of color and light.

"And what is he painting instead?"

"I don't really know, but the other day I saw one of his paintings, the figure of a woman clad in a sari, standing with her back to us, her face out of view, a long staircase rising endlessly in front of her."

I felt miserable listening to Sebati tell me the latest news about Afzal. I tried to recall his features, but I could not. I hadn't seen him in weeks, since I hardly ever stood on the veranda anymore. Does he have a mustache? How long is his hair? It didn't matter anymore. It wasn't worth it to me what I'd suffer if I slept with him again. And really, what difference did it make to whom I was married? Haroon or Afzal, Karim, or Rashid? My situation wouldn't be any different. A wife is like a buffalo circling a mill, her nose to the same grindstone, day in and day out. At least in loving Afzal without marriage, I had escaped that tyranny. Desire led me to him. In the end, I mortgaged my body to Afzal in order to purchase power.

When night fell, Haroon again lay beside me, rubbing his face on my stomach, inspecting my bosom to see if there were any more red marks. "You're not allowed to eat hilsa fish, or else my child will break out in rashes," he repeated. Every day now, he arranged for me to have chicken soup, four eggs and half a pint of milk. He wouldn't let me refuse, insisting it was doctor's orders. Now I ate first, finishing my meal before the men sat down. Haroon wanted to be sure I got the best.

I knew all the food was doing my figure no good. In my own eyes, I was gross, but nourishment was necessary for the healthy development of the child in my womb, and Haroon knew that. He had never before shown any interest in what I ate, but now he was like a mother hen. At night he fondled me with so much feeling, it continually took me by surprise. I had no idea he could be such a sensitive lover. I felt engulfed in the intensity of his emotion. "Tell me," I asked one night. "Tell me, what do you want? A boy or a girl?"

"I'll accept your gift with gratitude," he said solemnly, holding me in his arms. "A boy or a girl. It does not matter."

I was not convinced. I knew Haroon, like nearly every other man I knew, hoped for a boy. Who could ignore the advantages of being born male? As an oldest son, Haroon enjoyed unlimited freedom and opportunity, while Dolon lived under the limitations imposed on women—the limitations that still bound me. I had allowed this fetus to be conceived in a flash of anger. Yes, there was pleasure too, but not in the spirit of my girlhood dreams. I was not at peace. This child was a protest, a way of taking revenge, and its being was infused with the pain and suffering of all the women I knew.

Haroon was missing work with alarming frequency. "Oh darling," he would say, "I've taken the afternoon off. Shall we drive out into the country? To the river bank?" We went out at night; we dined at Aunt Sahedi's. And we took long walks in the early evening. The doctor had advised plenty of activity, and exercise to keep my muscles toned. And of course I had to rest. Haroon made me lie down so he could press his ear against my belly and listen for the tiny heartbeat. He was thrilled when the baby began to move. He'd kiss my stomach and sing out to the creature within, "Oh, my little darling, it's your daddy!" This made me laugh and laugh.

"Why are you so amused?" he asked me one day.

"Because you are such an eager father!"

Haroon had begun to count the months until the child's arrival, and pretty soon he was computing weeks and days and even hours. He filled the house with baby clothes and bottles, stuffed animals and baby powders and creams.

"Tell me what you want, darling!" he would say impatiently. I told him I wanted to go home to see my parents, but instead, he invited them over, setting Amma to prepare a feast, driving to Wari himself to pick them up. Of course I was happy when Mama and Baba and Nupur arrived and happy that Haroon insisted we have time alone together, but I was going mad sitting in the house all day. The pregnancy only emphasized the narrow limits of my life.

I wished I could have gone to them, but I was happy to see my family and embraced them all, breathing in my mother's wonderful smell as I had when I was a little girl.

"Do I look like myself?" I asked as they stared at my belly.

"Of course you don't," Nupur said.

"But I never said I wouldn't become pregnant!"

Nupur smiled weakly, and I could see that Mama was struggling to keep from weeping. My father just looked glum. I had left them a lithe young girl, and now I was grossly overweight even for a pregnant woman, out of breath at the slightest exertion. I had become a cartoon of the *bou* of the house. It was bad enough that marriage had taken me away from them, but they had not expected it would so deeply change me. One minute I was glad to see them, the next I was filled with rage.

"What's the matter?" I snapped. "Why do you look so unhappy? I am pregnant and my husband is a rich man who looks after me well and will take care of my child!"

"Stop pretending," Nupur retorted.

"Do you think I don't love you, just because I haven't come to see you?" Now I was trying to keep from crying, but I could not. I threw myself into my mother's arms and wept uncontrollably. I was so ashamed. Baba and Ma had made sacrifices to send me to school and university and they had always encouraged me. And here I was, my brain turning idle. I had no life of my own. I remembered the many times I heard Baba and Ma say with pride, "She will become a brilliant scientist. She will take care of us when we are old." Just like a son would. I couldn't stop weeping, looking at Baba, his proud and dignified face. I remembered how he'd sold our land in Bikrampur for a song rather than ask for a penny from his relatives. How he had always remained true to his beliefs, never straying from his true self. Now he and Ma lived on his pension. It was a modest life, but I had a father who would never acknowledge even the most difficult hardship.

"I wasn't educated like you. I did not have your opportunities." Ma said. She was stroking my hair as she had when I was little. "But my darling, I don't understand why you stay at home so much."

"I'm pregnant, Mama." She let me go and smiled sadly.

"Pregnancy is no excuse," she said gently.

We were sitting in the elegant front parlor, and though my family was polite, I could tell they weren't impressed, even though our house in Wari was almost shabby in comparison. In Wari, when I was a child, we had a rich next door neighbor, and, once when I saw him leave in his great big car, I commented to Baba that he must be a very important man. Baba immediately corrected me. "Not important, just rich." I, of course, envied the clothes the rich man's daughters wore and said so, but Baba did not soften. "Who says expensive clothes make one pretty? Your distinction lies within yourself. You will have wisdom and someday you will have learning. Beauty will come when you become beautiful in your attitude and behavior."

Another time when I was thirteen, I came home crying because some boys had pulled at my dress, and Baba took me aside and said, "Don't think that just because you're a girl, you're a lesser being. Walk with your head high, keep your backbone straight, and stand up for yourself."

With all his urging, Nupur and I had become spirited young women. But what had happened? Now we were both incarcerated in marriages, and Baba, in spite of his progressive ideas, had encouraged me to marry Haroon. I supposed that he could be forgiven for underestimating the barbarity of marriage—he never treated Ma badly. I had grown up knowing that a woman took her husband's name in marriage, but I did not imagine that my independence of spirit would disappear as well. Sebati was not Doctor Sebati at the clinic, but Mrs. Anwar. My obstetrician had no idea I had a degree in physics, though she knew very well that I was the wife of Haroon Ur Rashid, that my husband had an office in Motijheel, and she was well informed about the business he ran. As for the woman called Jhumur, she didn't know her at all!

Amma summoned us to dinner and Haroon himself served the rice. At the table, instead of being amused when Amma encouraged me to eat more, I was embarrassed. When Amma declared to my mother that she and Abba loved me like a daughter, Ma smiled, but I could see she was just playing along. Haroon glanced at me from time to time to see if I was suitably impressed by the delicious korma his mother had cooked, but I felt awkward. My in-laws were putting themselves out to honor my family, but I was sure they weren't planning to invite them back any time soon. How I longed for the kitchen in Wari and my mother's simple cooking—rice with *kajali* fish and dried red chillies.

It was decided that the family car and driver would take my family home. Leaning against the door, as I watched Ma and Baba and Nupur leave, my thoughts drifted again to the days when Baba had insisted I stand on my own two feet, when he declared money was not the key to a good life. In spite of having grown up in such an enlightened atmosphere, I now seemed helpless in the face of old superstitions and attitudes about women. Baba had told me to marry Haroon or stop seeing him, but he certainly hadn't expected that I would turn into the bloated pregnant *bou* who now disappeared into darkness as she waved goodbye.

After they left, Haroon gave me an accounting of how much the dinner had cost—the shops where he'd bought the fish and meat, the most excellent fish and meat that could be found anywhere. I was stunned to be reminded how much money meant to him. I recalled that when we first discussed marriage, it was Haroon who wanted to know how much money my family would ask that he pay. I remember he had been shocked when I said, "Not a penny!" Haroon had been stunned. "But the woman's family always gets money!"

"But we aren't marrying for money, are we?" I was laughing. "We're marrying because we love each other. Think about it. Do you think I'd ask for a refund if our relationship broke down?" Needless to say, Haroon was very happy when I said these things. He took my hand and rubbed it against his cheek.

"You're different from other girls—that's why I love you so much!" He was practically in tears, moved I now realize, because he didn't have to dole out any money. "I want you for myself," he kept repeating. "Just for myself."

"We are two different people, my darling." I'd corrected him then. "Each with an independent mind. I am not your property, any more than you are mine."

Memory of those days, when my back was firm and straight and my mind as free as the air, brightened my spirits like fragments of light from a full moon.

Haroon had me admitted to a birth clinic in the Gulshan district, and not in Dhanmundi. "The care is better there," he said. He took unlimited leave from the office and stayed at my bedside. It started to seem as if he himself was about to give birth. He kept busy making me eat, sit, walk, and sleep. He bought linens for the bassinet, bottles for feeding, and summoned specialists and nurses to my bedside. Relatives paraded through my room and Aunt Sahedi lectured me on how to cope with labor. Amma tied a good luck charm around my arm and wrote out a prayer for me to recite. She looked terribly anxious—but the amulet and prayer were not for my health, but for the well-being of Haroon's child.

Like my husband and his family, I became enchanted by the promise of this child; all I could think of was a baby lying on my belly, the smell of it, the softness of its skin. I would no longer need to beg for love, I would have my child.

Haroon was always agitated when the doctor came in the evening. "Are mother and child all right?" he would ask over and over. "Is everything OK? Will she need a caesarean?" The doctor confronted this buffoonery deadpan, not knowing what to say. Haroon would follow him to the door, and stop chattering only when the doctor, fed up, turned and scolded him. "How many times must I repeat that everything is fine?" Nevertheless Haroon ran for him at my slightest sigh. This compulsive attention made me furious. "Why are you so anxious?" I felt like asking. "This isn't your child I'm carrying. You destroyed what was yours with your own hands—now you are showering your love on a creature who has no relation to you, in whose conception you played no part!"

I did require a caesarean. I gave birth to a male child at three o'clock in the morning, after an excruciating labor. Haroon was ecstatic. He all but tore the infant from the nurse's arms and then held him wrapped in an embroidered *kantha* close to his chest. It gave me pleasure to see this, but sleep pulled at me, and dreams, reminding me I had forgotten nothing. Not the scooping out in bits and pieces of the fetus, not the pain afterward, not my sorrow. Nor had I forgotten how I had implored my supposedly devoted husband not to destroy what was ours, or how he had turned his eyes toward me, cold and expressionless as marble. "The child is yours!" I'd shouted over and over. I can still hear the sound of the sharp metal instruments invading my womb, though it's not the doctor I see, but Haroon. He is wet with sweat, bleary-eyed, wearing a garish, toothy smile as he pokes with grim determination at the walls of my uterus. I ask him to stop. I tell him I am in pain, but he carries on. He's not only yanking at the fetus, but at my uterus and vagina. Sharp contraptions dig into my belly and slice through my face, my eyes, and my brain. I can't prevent it. My head throbs with excruciating pain and I cry out for tranquilizers.

When I wake up, I find myself in a new room on a bed with fresh sheets. Haroon is sitting on another bed holding the newborn. Amma, Dolon, Ranu, and the aunts surround him. "He has Haroon's nose and forehead!" Aunt Sahedi exclaims.

"Not only that," Amma adds, "but also his arms and legs!"

"But what about his lips?" Dolon asks, and Ranu quickly answers.

"Haroon's lips were plucked from his face and set right here!" Somaiya is so thrilled to have a baby cousin, she can hardly keep still. She wants to touch him, but her mother won't let her. Amma claims the baby will, of course, have legs as long as his father's, and Haroon lifts the quilt to take a look.

My eyes are now wide open. Haroon brings my son to me, his face beaming with fatherly pride. He holds him close to my face, and I catch a flash of a miniature Afzal in the child's expression. I'd blocked Afzal's face from my mind, but the baby's face brings him back. I want to take the infant in my arms, but Haroon tells me that I should be careful. I have to sit up, wash my hands with warm water and soap, place a fresh *kantha* on my lap. I've never held a child so small and I'm afraid he will slip through my fingers. The baby cries, draws his lips into a thin line, reminding me of Afzal's mouth ready for a kiss! Haroon presses close to me, staring at the baby with captive eyes.

"Everybody says he looks like me!"

"You wanted that, didn't you?"

"Of course he looks like me! He's my flesh and blood."

I smile ironically, which Haroon takes to mean I'm asserting the baby looks like me as well.

"His ears are like yours," he concedes, but he's not willing to give me any more credit.

Already there's a gold chain around the baby's neck. Now, Haroon insists I breast-feed and I take the baby into my arms, pull away my nightgown and feed him as Haroon and everyone else watches. The room is crowded with the family and with doctors and nurses, and Habib is passing a plate of pastry and sweets.

In the evening, Haroon's friends visit, laden with gifts, toys, baby soaps, creams, and shampoos. Some bring a gold ring or chain, but my mother brings tiny linen vests—she is too poor to buy gold, which, I can tell, disappoints Haroon. Of course he is not content with just sweets either. He's promised a *biryani* feast to celebrate my return from the hospital—I'm here a few extra days to recover from the caesarean and still in some pain, but Haroon himself nurses and bathes me, changes the baby's diapers, applies ointment to my wound, takes care of everything. I sleep through the night, but Haroon can't close his eyes, even for a second. I had wanted Nupur to come stay with me, but Haroon wouldn't hear of it. He's the father, he says, and welcomes the work that accompanies this joyous occasion. Looking at his tired, sleepless yet smiling eyes, I wonder why it is I don't feel guilty at my deception.

When we come home from the hospital, the house is decked with flowers to welcome the newborn, and one by one, relatives arrive to take a look. They bring more gifts and the house is filled with singing and dancing. In spite of myself, I revel in the attention. I'm no longer the veiled daughter-in-law who hovers quietly passing the tea tray. I am the mother of the precious scion of the family. In my absence the house has been adorned to a degree that no daughter's birth would have inspired. To welcome this boy child, a buffalo is slaughtered to feed the relatives, the neighbors, everyone we know. Haroon names his son Mahboob, and of course bestows him with his family surname, Ur Rashid. I am Jhumur Zeenat Sultana, but my son is not called Mahboob Ur Sultana.

"Let me give him his pet name," I insist.

"And what will that be?"

"Ananda,"

"Okay then," Haroon laughs. "Ananda it will be!" I laugh, too, and Haroon kisses me on the lips. "You've done me proud," he says.

"How?"

"By giving me the gift of a son."

I pity Haroon. I watch Sebati and Anwar moving around the room, helping to look after the guests. Wiping perspiration from her brow, Sebati comes toward me. "I'm jealous!" she says. I look at her and am about to reassure her that someday she will have a child when she surprises me. "I didn't realize Haroon loved you so much!"

"He loves his son, not me."

"Can't be," she insists. "He wouldn't be so mad for the child if he didn't care for you." We talk about all kinds of things, and finally about Afzal. "He's gone away to Australia," she announces. Before I can think, I give a deep sigh. Sebati doesn't notice. "He left a painting behind," she says. I give a slight start. I wonder which one? The nude with long hair like mine, or the girl from South India?

"It's the one with a girl standing, her back to us, facing a long flight of stairs," she says, as though I had uttered my question aloud. "I asked Afzal who she was, and he said 'No one.'"

"How do I look?" Sebati asks me. She is wearing a dark green sari of sheer figured muslin and has placed a green dot on her forehead.

"You look lovely, but you always do." She leans toward me and pinches my cheek. "Not as good looking as you, my dear. It's not for nothing Haroon is crazy about you!" I push her hand away and smile.

"I'm a mother now. I have no time for Haroon's antics." And then I take the baby in my arms and begin to breastfeed him as Sebati watches, her eyes wide with envy.

"Your husband loves you," I say.

"Of course he does. He's given me this new sari to wear tonight. It shows, doesn't it, how much he cares for me?"

"But does even the most beautiful sari constitute love?"

"Yes," she insists. "One gives unstintingly if one is in love.

When one feels intensely, one wants to give everything—money, inheritance, all that one has."

Dolon arrives late.

She insists Anis will join her, believing that I know nothing of what has happened to him. "What can I say?" Dolon says. "He's invested so much and he has to be so careful. His business will collapse if he doesn't pay the closest attention. He sent me some money yesterday." Beads of perspiration have gathered on her brow.

I wipe them away, asking her, as warmly as I can, "And what will you do with the money, Dolon?"

"Buy something for Ananda, of course."

"That is entirely unnecessary." I feel so sorry for her, knowing what I do about the actual state of her life. "Buy something for yourself."

The next morning Haroon finally goes back to work. I know how much he resents having to be away from Ananda. He calls, it seems, every half hour to ask what his child is doing. "He's asleep." "He's nursing." "He's in Habib's arms." "Amma is changing his diapers." Even Hasan rocks this child, and several times a day everyone in turn grabs the phone to tell Haroon what his wondrous son is now doing. "He's smiling!" "He's lifting his right arm." Everyone is involved in his baths, his naps and his meals. Everyone that is, but me.

A few days after we return from the clinic, Ranu races in to tell me that she and Hasan have arranged to go to Saudi Arabia after all.

"Our life has completely turned around," she says.

"Why do you say that?" I'm suspicious of this new plan.

"Hasan will go first, and I will follow."

"And you won't miss us?"

"Why should I? I'm looking forward to a place of our own. It's comfortable here with the family—I don't have to worry about where to sleep, or what to eat, but I'll breathe more easily in my own house, no matter how modestly we have to live." Ranu is still in her teens. I was bouncing balls in Wari at her age and here she is talking like a woman of the world.

"So Ranu," I ask her, lowering my voice. "Does Hasan love you?"

Ranu puckers her lips. "Love? What does one need that for! I want a home, and children. I dream of a house to decorate as I like, of waiting for my husband to come home in the evening."

"And that's enough? If you don't care about love, don't you long for passion?"

"I have had passion. For love and passion, I skipped school and went to the movies with Hasan. Then I dressed in my elder sister's clothes and sat down as his bride."

"Do you mean to tell me that during the ceremony you sat while Hasan stood up?" Ranu bursts out laughing. "In actual fact, we both sat down at the office of the justice of the peace and got married, but where I live, you say a girl 'sits down' to marry and a boy 'takes a bride!'"

"Why is that? It seems strange to me."

"Because girls stay at home and boys go out to work," Ranu says, as if stating the obvious, and then she laughs some more.

I feel like having a serious talk with her. "Ranu, get out!" I'd say. "Leave this dreary situation behind. Read. Study. Make something of yourself!" But I know she's not interested. Once she asked me what she had to gain by getting a college degree, and I had no convincing answer. She'd left school after seventh grade and I hold a degree in physics, but we both run a man's household.

In the house, there is still a festive feeling in the air, even though the carnival has come to an end. Balloons still hang from the ceiling and the kitchen is overflowing with food, which is lucky because visitors continue to drop by. Soon, though, the days resume their normal rhythm and again I hear Dolon's muffled sobs when I wake in the middle of the night. Amma returns to worrying about Hasan and Anis, and I am back in the kitchen cooking, handing off Ananda to others. My father-in-law grows grimmer by the day, and then one morning Amma asks if I've heard anything from Chittagong. Anis is still in prison for smuggling, and now that the baby is born, she had expected Haroon to go there to see about bailing him out.

"I've heard nothing about Chittagong," I tell her.

"But Haroon said he'd see about the bail."

"He speaks to me of nothing but his son. I can't imagine he'll leave Ananda even for an hour," I tell her, returning to chopping vegetables for supper.

"But *bhabi*, he has to . . . Anis is his brother-in-law, his sister's husband." Out the window, Habib is strolling the garden, the baby in his arms. "And," Amma says, "he has to think about Habib, too. The boy hasn't taken his exams." I go outside and take the baby from his youngest uncle's arms.

"So, Habib, what's the news about your studies?"

"They're in the doldrums," he says with a grin.

"And your music, has that also come to an end?"

"No," he says, "of course not *bhabi*. And have I told you the name of our group? Different Touch! Isn't that great?"

"Why do all the boys give their bands English names nowadays?"

Habib laughs, wriggling his slim body like some creeping plant. "You talk as if you live in a different era! *Bhabi*, are you feeling like an old lady?"

"I'm a mother now."

"Don't pamper Habib about his singing," Amma interjects. "Tell him to study and become a man."

Suddenly Amma values my opinion! Suddenly I'm considered wise, not silly! That's why the rent from downstairs now comes straight to me. Haroon has seen to that. He tells me the money is for household expenses. I am now the person who does all the shopping, makes the menus, supervises the cooking.

"If you don't study, Habib, Haroon will banish you to another country."

"Oh *bhabi*, don't let him do that! The band is finally successful! You'll see. I will become someone someday."

Later Amma thanks me for taking Habib to task, but Haroon pays no attention when she pleads with him to go to Chittagong, to see after Hasan, or to set Habib straight. His attention is entirely absorbed by little Ananda. He has hired a twelve-year-old girl to take care of his son—to wash his diapers, warm his milk, bathe him, and above all, to see that he doesn't fall out of bed in his sleep. In spite of the fact that Ananda is just weeks old and cannot yet play, he's gotten him a car that you wind up and a talking doll. It is Haroon who rises at night when the baby cries and changes him, he who takes him out in the stroller in the late afternoon when he comes home from work.

"It seems that Ananda is all yours and not mine at all," I protest. Haroon smiles, a smile of satisfaction. I've taken to calling him "Ananda's Baba" adopting the family form of address, and Haroon is pleased as punch. When I shout "Ananda's Baba, where have you gone?" or "Come here Ananda's Baba!" his eyes light up with pride.

Everywhere he goes, he finds an excuse to take Ananda with him, showing the baby's marvelous accomplishments to anyone who expresses the slightest interest. These days Haroon no longer lifts Somaiya and whirls her in his arms, and she sits silent and forlorn, watching her uncle, completely besotted, play with his infant son. It gives me some satisfaction to see the family so upended. And I am also happy in my own secret way to see how much Haroon loves our little Ananda.

Time passes before we know what has happened, disappearing like a flock of birds rises into the sky, never to return. If I am being poetic, please accept my apologies. Time passes, free-flowing, unlike the lives of mothers and daughters, of wives and mothers-in-law, women who live confined within the walls of kitchens and nurseries, inhabiting lives that they have not chosen, or have chosen unaware.

Sleeping, I stretch a hand toward Ananda, and suddenly I'm awake. I am about to shake Haroon from sleep and ask him where our child has gone, but then I remember that Ananda is one year old now and sleeps in Amma's room, in a bed of his own.

More time passes and soon he is at nursery school in the neighborhood. He's no longer small—he can walk and run and talk and paint, and even, placing a small finger on a letter, begin to distinguish words. Haroon's happiness has not diminished in the slightest, and because of his diligent teaching, he has been rewarded. Even before he was able to say "Ma," Ananda called for his father, "Baba." And then,

"Baba is eating." "Baba is walking." And "I want Baba's lap." Haroon, of course, was ecstatic. To honor his intense love for his son, he has changed the name of his business from Modern Traders to Ananda Trading.

Much has changed in our household these three years of Ananda's short life. Haroon's father died of a heart attack, Hasan and Ranu have left for Saudi Arabia, and Habib has given up Different Touch and gotten a job. Dolon is divorced and she and Somaiya have come to live with us. I still hear Dolon's cries at night; I fear she is slowly losing her mind. She talks to herself, rips apart Somaiya's school books and throws them into pails of water. One day in a fit, she tossed Ananda's gold chain out the window. Amma weeps most of the time, sits for hours praying, hands lifted to the sky. Sebati and her husband have left the apartment downstairs and others have moved in—a middle-aged couple with two sons and four daughters. Before she left, Sebati came to see me. She'd heard from Afzal, she said. He'd married an Australian girl, taken citizenship there, and was contented. Sebati transferred from Dhaka Medical College to a hospital in Mymensingh in the north and Anwar was working for a nongovernmental organization headquartered near Chittagong.

I too have changed. I no longer keep my head covered and I go out alone if I have to, to shop, roam the city, or travel to Wari to see my parents and sister. Often I spend the day with Shipra or get together with my old friends, Nadira, Chandana, Subhash, and Arzu. Chandana is married now and Nadira has decided to remain single. Subhash is still considering marriage, but he is busy looking after his family. He tutors for a living because he hasn't yet found a full-time job. Arzu is working in his father's firm.

For many years we hadn't gotten together as a group, so one day, I suggest to Haroon that we invite my friends for a reunion dinner.

"Your friends?"

"Yes, my friends."

"Which friends?"

I look at him with steady eyes and say without a trace of emotion. "You remember them! My college friends and the boys I knew in Wari—Subhash, Nadira, Chandana, and Arzu."

"Oh yes, of course!" And we invite them and ransack the best markets, buying up the freshest fish and lamb, the most luscious produce, and sweets of the highest quality. Rosuni and Sakhina set about chopping and cooking. It will be a sumptuous feast! Haroon dons a fresh panjabi and pyjama and sprinkles himself with cologne, and I wear a white sari with a red border and a gardenia in my hair. As we await our guests, I can only smile, brushing aside all the years of heartache. My husband greets my old friends with a broad smile. Despite our long separation, my ties with these friends have not weakened, and I sit down with them, lighthearted. When I explain that it was I, not Haroon, who was responsible for the long silence, they relax and laugh as if he too were their old friend. Happily, we eat together, falling into gales of laughter as we remember the days at college and childhood in Wari. When I see a trace of sadness cross Subhash's face, I want to ask him about his brother Sujit's death, but I do not because I don't want to break the spell.

Everyone believed Sujit had died in an automobile accident, but my father told me the real story. Sujit had gone alone to kick a football on the grounds of Armanitola, the high school near the Star Mosque. A couple of boys who looked familiar called to him and then grabbed him and took him to the entrance of the mosque. "Why have you brought me here?" Sujit asked. In one voice, the boys responded, "Because you are an infidel." Sujit turned and began to run, but the boys caught up with him, dragged him to the river, and there, throngs of young men emerged from the darkness and hacked him to death. I am deep in the horror of that moment, when the laughter of my friends brings me back, and I turn to Subhash, "Don't forget your friends after you marry!"

"Subhash's marriage isn't taking place, my dear!" Chandana said. "Haven't you heard? The dastardly Mina has disappeared!"

"After such a long courtship?" Subhash had been completely besotted with her, and Mina seemed to return his affections. "Well, clearly she doesn't deserve such devotion," I said, trying to repair my faux pas. I had tried to cheer Subhash, but had succeeded only in bringing up another painful subject. He hadn't told me anything of his brother's death or that his mother, Kakima, who had lived with us all those years, was suffering from cancer. I look at my dear friend and still see the young boy he was when I first knew him. "Don't leave us, Subhash," I say to myself. "The river that flows through our city may be sullied with Sujit's blood, but there is love for you here with us."

Click. Arzu has picked up his new camera and caught me in my reverie. Subhash is embarrassed and makes Arzu click again because he thinks he looked awful in the first shot, and then Arzu says, "Haroonbhai, go embrace your wife." Haroon does so. "I want you both smiling," Arzu says, and we do. Smile. Click. And Arzu clicks on and on and then Chandana rushes out for Ananda and puts him on our laps, and, click, lo and behold, the image of a happy family! And click again, and, with one arm holding Ananda and the other around Haroon, I am the smiling wife of an equally smiling husband and the smiling mother of his son. Click. Click. I ask Arzu to give the camera to Haroon.

"Now you take some," I say, and I stand among my old friends, leaning against Chandana, putting my arm around Arzu. Haroon, the dutiful husband, shows no irritation whatsoever. Perhaps he thinks I am at last indissolubly tied to his family, a bond effected by the joining of our blood in the veins of our child.

But what I want my husband to witness here tonight is the embrace of my dearest friends, women and men who have known me since childhood, friends who know where I began my life. I watch Ananda move from one lap to another as we joke and sing old songs. I want Haroon to appreciate what my friends mean to me, to understand that there is precious life outside the bonds of one's family. When everyone has eaten and tea has been served, I stand up and interrupt the flow of conversation around me, arguments about the economy and trade, jobs, society, and the family. "My friends, my husband," I say. "I have something of importance to announce. Something that may take you by surprise."

There is sudden silence as everyone turns to look at me.

"I have a slip of paper in my hand," I declare, unfurling it like a scroll. "What do you think it is?"

"I have no idea," Haroon says, beginning to laugh.

"Let me try to guess," Chandana says. "Something to do with the marriage ceremony?"

Now Nadira starts to laugh. "I say it's a divorce declaration!"

"Wrong again," I reply.

"Have you taken to writing poetry?" Subhash asks.

"A speech by Lenin?" Arzu asks. In college, he was the Marxist, I, the Maoist.

"Close," I say, laughing. "It is a letter I've written accepting a job."

Now everyone falls silent. "I will be teaching at Bhikharunisa Noon's primary school, starting tomorrow morning." Everyone claps except for Haroon, but I continue my announcement. "Don't imagine getting this job was easy. I had to apply, go for an interview, and take an exam."

"You've done all of this without letting anyone know?" Haroon asks.

I lean in and give him a kiss, right on the mouth. "Yes, my dear. I did all this in utter secret."

The party lasts well past midnight, and when we have put our boy back in Amma's room and are comfortably in bed, Haroon asks, "Why didn't you tell me about the job?"

"I wanted to surprise you."

"And do you think I was surprised?"

"I could tell you were taken aback," I say. I am relieved he's smiling. "And weren't you also thinking there were many other things I might be doing without your knowledge?"

At that Haroon goes silent. "You didn't let me work after we were married," I say softly, "which was a slap in the face. Now after a few years, I have surprised you by taking a job. It is like slapping you back."

"Is that so?" Haroon replies carefully. "And how do you plan to work with a three-year-old son? Who will take him to school? Who will bring him home?"

"I will take him to school, and some days I will bring him back. You will, too. And so will Habib, if need be."

"And who will feed him? And shop for food?"

It intrigues me that Haroon is not saying I can't go to work. He won't, it seems, prevent me from working. It seems such a long time ago he had those fits of jealousy, I can hardly remember that expressionless, marblelike countenance. And, clearly, he no longer thinks of me as a helpless woman.

"Ananda is not only your son," I say now. "He is mine as well. I am as concerned about his welfare as you are." Haroon turns his face toward the window.

"Are you short of cash?" he asks after a moment.

"Of course not. You give me plenty."

"So?"

"That's your money—not mine. I want to find out how it feels to earn money of my own, what it's like to spend my own money on what I want. And I want to give money to others, even to you and Ananda and to my parents. I want to take responsibility as you do."

It is clear to Haroon that I will now live life on my own terms. I will not be like the people he employs who don't speak up or look him in the eye. I will no longer be the kind of wife who is beholden, a mere servant.

I can see this new state of things has agitated Haroon. He is turning in bed. He cannot sleep.

As I lie awake beside him, I watch day break through my familiar window and think to myself, I am finally Haroon's wife, but not his slave. I stay with him to fulfill a human need for love and companionship, but I have no actual need, just because I am a woman, to dust and sweep, no obligation to breed and rear children.

I could not talk back to Haroon if I was dependent on his financial largesse. As much as I admired my father, I now take a different position from his on the necessity of marriage. Why is it not possible for a man and woman to spend time together without being married? Even to live together without marriage? If I had I spent more time with Haroon before we married, I would have seen the side of him that hurt me so much, even perhaps made a different choice.

The early morning sun falls on me, and despite an entirely sleepless night, I feel wonderfully refreshed. After breakfast, I drop Ananda at his kindergarten and take a tonga to my place of employment, the school on Bailey Road. I sit in the principal's office and sign the register, then listen to her description of my new job. I am happy and I feel a new kind of strength. I am someone, separate and distinct from the wife of Haroon, mother of Ananda, *bou* of Amma, *bhabi* of Dolon, Hasan, and Habib, daughter of my parents and sister of Nupur. I am Zeenat Sultana, Jhumur, a teacher. I am finished with a life of submission, and my husband knows I will no longer stand for his cruelty.

I do not harbor any regret for the manner in which I brought Ananda into the world. I took the opportunity to avenge the loss of my first child and the indignity I'd suffered as a woman. But my heart lifts with happiness when I leave for work and Haroon takes Ananda in his arms, when our son calls to Baba as often as he calls to Mama. I have taken back my life and doused the fires of suspicion and jealousy that raged so fiercely in my husband's heart they left my own heart charred. In the years since the birth of my son, I have been bathed with a contentment I could never have imagined.